'You wa...
Riley bi...

Allison reali... ...ay she died, but he'd never offer what she yearned for. 'And you want too little.' The end was near, she knew. All over again. 'Every time you get too close to caring, you back away.'

'Be glad I do,' Riley said angrily, knowing he had to make her want to leave. 'I never pretended with you.' All this time with her, and she still didn't understand that he didn't have the right stuff! Not for her. Not for her little son, Devin. What she wanted from him meant loving. Loving so much he'd have to face the inadequacies he'd always run from.

'Loving means giving, sharing,' she said, her voice cracking with emotion.

Riley stood before her, his expression unreadable.

But his silence…

His silence seemed to say it all.

Dear Reader

It's August—the height of summer—and we have some truly sizzling, satisfying reads in the Special Edition™ line-up!

This month, the always-delightful Joan Elliott Pickart brings you our THAT'S MY BABY! title; *Texas Baby* is the final book in her FAMILY MEN series, where the forty-something heroine rediscovers the joy of motherhood when she adopts a precious baby girl. But the dashing man of her dreams has no intention of playing daddy again...

An uncle's will looks set to cause trouble for the McKendrick siblings in Cathy Gillen Thacker's HASTY WEDDINGS. It starts with *The Cowboy's Bride*, when Cody is forced to re-marry the woman who ran out on him just hours after their elopement and *before the wedding night!*

Also this month, fate reunites a family in *A Daddy for Devin* by Jennifer Mikels, and passion flares between a disgruntled cowboy and a tough lady cop in *The Cop and the Cradle* by Suzannah Davis—the second of the SWITCHED AT BIRTH books.

We finish off the month with secret-baby and amnesia stories from Phyllis Halldorson and Judith Yates. Look out for *The Millionaire's Baby* and *Brother of the Groom*.

Happy reading!

The Editors

A Daddy for Devin

JENNIFER MIKELS

All the characters in this book have no existence outside the imagination
of the author, and have no relation whatsoever to anyone bearing the same
name or names. They are not even distantly inspired by any individual
known or unknown to the author, and all the incidents are pure invention.

First published in Great Britain 1998
Silhouette Books, Eton House, 18-24 Paradise Road,
Richmond, Surrey TW9 1SR

© Suzanne Kuhlin 1998

ISBN 0 373 24150 X

23-9808

Printed and bound in Spain
by Litografía Rosés S.A., Barcelona

For Michael and Trina
and especially for Bradley, an inspiration
in his own special way.

JENNIFER MIKELS

is from Chicago, Illinois, but resides now in Phoenix,
Arizona, with her husband, two sons and a shepherd-collie.
She enjoys reading, sports, antiques and long walks.
Though she's done technical writing in public relations, she
loves writing romances and happy endings.

Other novels by Jennifer Mikels

Silhouette Special Edition®

A Sporting Affair
Whirlwind
Remember the Daffodils
Double Identity
Stargazer
Freedom's Just Another Word
A Real Charmer
A Job for Jack
Your Child, My Child
Denver's Lady
Jake Ryker's Back in Town
Sara's Father
Child of Mine
Expecting: Baby
Remember Me?

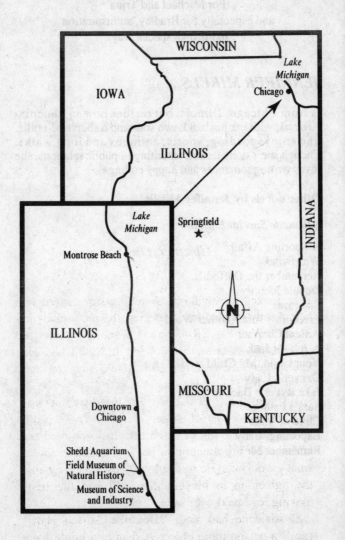

Chapter One

She looked breathtaking. A setting sun danced on her slightly tousled hair, catching the red strands in its rays. With ease, Riley could drum up the feel of its coppery softness, could smell it. Smell her. He knew every inch of her body. He'd touched and tasted it; he'd worshiped it.

He wanted to feel nothing, but that was impossible. Silvery wisps of straps curled over her bare shoulders; black silk caressed her hips, skimmed her knees, drew his attention to her legs veiled in sheer, smoky stockings. He took a long, slow breath against the tightening in his gut. She still had the best-looking legs he'd ever seen.

If someone had said, "Describe Allison Harrigan," a person more objective than him might have used words like *punctual, dependable, disciplined*. It was a bland description, to Riley's way of thinking. *Vibrant, funny, sensitive* suited her better. *Sexy, bewitching, breathtaking.* Yeah, definitely breathtaking.

Around him, guests arrived at the Somersets' suburban, palatial home for what society columnists in all the Chicago newspapers had proclaimed the wedding of the year.

For another moment, Riley soaked in the sight of her. The last few days they'd been together, he'd been withdrawn. A phone call from his sister had triggered the foul mood. He hadn't heard from Cindy in years, then out of the blue she'd asked him to fly to see her in Texas. He hadn't been able to explain anything to Allie. No, that was wrong. He hadn't wanted to.

She'd been upset with him, but he couldn't tell her what was wrong. He'd been having enough trouble dealing with the unexpected call from his sister.

He and Alice hadn't parted in anger. She'd quietly, calmly announced that she'd wanted more than he was willing to give. She wanted marriage, kids. And he'd known then what he'd avoided thinking about during the six months they'd been living together: he had to push her away before he ruined her life.

"Mr. Garrison, Mr. Vincetti is looking for you."

Riley focused on the Somersets' butler. "Thanks, Charles. Where is he?"

"He's waiting in the kitchen for the nuptials to begin."

Poor Nick. Stuck in the Somerset kitchen with the temperamental cook, who probably was fighting for territorial rights with the hired caterer.

Crossing the manicured lawn at the back of the house, Riley sidestepped the bride's cousin, a daffy blonde who was expounding to another guest about the benefits of a kale diet, and wound his way around other guests to enter the kitchen. A harried-looking caterer only glanced his way.

Looking like the stereotypical nervous groom, Nick Vincetti was pacing around the kitchen table.

"Finally. I thought for sure you were going to be late."

"Relax," Riley said, amused by his friend's uncharacteristic show of nerves.

"You can say that. You're not getting married."

And never will, Riley mused, not moving away from the doorway.

"It's a damn circus, isn't it?" Nick braced a shoulder against the kitchen doorjamb to view new arrivals. "I don't think Ann knows who half these people are. Except for my family and guys at the precinct, I invited only a few friends and…" As he paused, Riley felt his stare. "Allie's here. Did you see her?"

More guests crossed the lush lawn to the rows of chairs beneath a white canopy, where Allison stood. Riley still couldn't take his eyes off her. He still ached for her, and damned himself for it. Too much emotion weakened a person. It was a hard-earned lesson learned eighteen years ago in his youth. One he'd forgotten only once, because of her.

"You haven't seen her in over two years. Why did you invite her?"

"I didn't know if she was coming. I sent the in-

vitation to her mother's house. You know me," Nick
said quickly. "I haven't had my head on straight for
weeks, so I didn't know if she'd sent back the
RSVP." He gave Riley a puzzled look. "Tell me it
didn't feel good seeing her again."

"What I feel doesn't matter. You did her no favor
by forcing this meeting." He heard the annoyance in
his voice and took a deep breath. Nick didn't deserve
this. "Fix that," Riley said about the boutonniere in
the lapel of Nick's tuxedo.

Nick adjusted the flower. "Do you have the
ring?"

"I've got the ring, Nick." Now wasn't the time to
think about him and Allie. This was Nick's day.
"Getting cold feet?"

"Not about marrying Ann," Nick was quick to
assure him. "Never that. But I'd rather walk down a
dark alley and face some drug-crazed kid," he muttered, sticking a finger in his collar and twisting his
neck against the confining restraint.

Some men were meant for marriage. Riley thought
Nick belonged with a wife and kids. "As your best
man, it's my job to get you out there—on time." In
all the years he'd worked with Nick in vice, and now
homicide, he'd never seen him so uptight. "Let's
go." He nudged him with his elbow. "There's a
beautiful woman waiting for you."

Following his friend toward the trellis of pink tea
roses, Riley glanced at Allie, sitting now in the last
row of chairs. Back straight, she fiddled with the
clasp of the small black purse in her lap. He knew
her well. She was nervous. Would she talk to him?

There was no reason to even question that. By nature, she was generous, open, forgiving.

Nick swung a look back at him, forcing Riley to a standstill. "Do you have the ring?"

"You asked me that already. I have it," Riley assured him. As he moved into position with Nick at the rose trellis, he let his gaze wander to her once more. Head bent, she seemed unaware of him. He'd never forgotten her. He'd had six months with her, months when she'd been too much a part of him. And two years to forget her, but he never had.

Allie glanced at her wristwatch. She'd left home only forty minutes ago, but she knew she'd never sit through the wedding ceremony unless she made a phone call first.

With a glance around, she spotted an austere-looking servant with gray hair and cornered him for directions about where to find a phone. She explicitly followed the ones he gave her, sure that if she didn't she'd get lost in the maze of rooms.

Inside a library with floor-to-ceiling bookshelves, she punched her home phone number. Through terrace doors, she watched guests who'd been milling around being ushered to seats.

"Allie?" her mother said as a greeting. "Why are you calling?"

"How is he?" Allie asked.

"He's fine."

"Is his fever down?"

"Yes. I told you he's fine." A slim woman with salt-and-pepper hair, her mother had been Allie's rock during some of the most unsettling days of her life. "You worry more than I do."

"It's called motherhood," Allie said with a laugh. During the sixteen months since Devin's birth, she'd worried about every bump he got, every tooth that had pushed through.

"I think you were right earlier about another tooth coming in."

"I hope so." Allie's concern stemmed from his having chronic ear infections. In a few days, he was scheduled to have tubes placed in his ears. Until then, she couldn't help fretting whenever he wasn't feeling well.

"The wedding hasn't started yet?"

"Soon." Allie glanced again toward the terrace doors. Almost all of the chairs were filled.

"Have you seen him?"

It amazed Allie that her mother had waited this long to discuss Riley. "Not yet." She knew Riley would be here. For days, she'd debated with herself about coming to the wedding, but she'd wanted to see Nick get married, to share in an old friend's happiness. The problem was he was Riley's friend, too. His closest friend. Chances were Riley would be Nick's best man at the wedding. She might believe she was tempting fate, but she'd learned he'd gotten involved with another woman soon after she'd left him. "I've got to go, Mom. I'll be home early."

"Don't rush."

Allie smiled. "Then I might stay awhile. Stefan won't be here until later."

"Stefan? You invited him?" her mother asked, not

veiling her disapproval. More than once she'd stated that his persnickety manner drove her crazy.

"Why shouldn't I have invited him?"

"You need a different kind of man in your life. Someone who knows how to have fun. Besides he has a girlfriend."

"I like routines, stability, orderliness," Allie reminded her.

"I know you do, but being with a man like that could make you very dull."

Allie couldn't help laughing. "Are you saying I'm dull?"

A smile colored her mother's voice. "No, sweetheart, you're not dull—yet. But he's too...well, it isn't healthy to be so punctual, so rigid."

"Yes, I know." Allie refrained from arguing. This was advice from a woman who never arrived anywhere on time. "I've got to go, Mom. Give Devin a kiss for me."

With a shake of her head, she set down the receiver and hurried back in the direction of her seat. She guessed what her mother was hoping for. If she saw Riley again, they might get back together. It wouldn't happen. Allie had already accepted that she'd closed that chapter in her life. He'd never lied to her. From the beginning of their relationship he'd given her no promises.

In passing, Allie smiled at Nick's mother, who was ready to be escorted to her seat. As unobtrusively as possible, Allie sank onto the chair she'd previously vacated.

That's when she saw Riley standing near the trellis

of flowers next to Nick. Tall, he had a lean, athletic body. Late afternoon sunlight shone on his dark blond hair, emphasizing lighter, sun-bleached streaks. His beard was gone, no longer masking a strong face with high, slashing cheekbones and hollows beneath them. Also gone was the long hair, though strands still brushed the back of the collar of his tuxedo.

She supposed she'd caused their breakup when she'd mentioned marriage. He'd said nothing. No words had been needed. He didn't want that kind of commitment.

Caught up in the euphoria of loving him, she'd willingly accepted what he'd offered. She'd blocked from her mind thoughts of a future. She'd refrained from pressing him for words of commitment. She'd even convinced herself that what they'd had was enough. It had been, until the nausea had hit suddenly one morning. Her hand had trembled as she'd taken the home pregnancy test. The result had forced her to face what she'd been dodging—she needed to think of the future.

So she'd left him, taking her secret with her. She hadn't doubted that he would have tried to do the right thing, make a commitment to her and the baby. But pride had kept her silent. She'd wanted him to want to marry her, not feel he had to.

During the next hour, Riley listened to his friends exchange vows, posed for pictures and mingled with guests. He danced with Nick's sisters, Bianca and

Mara, and he stayed beside the maid of honor, a sleek brunette, until her fiancé showed up.

As evening fell, lights sparkled on shrubbery around the terrace and gazebo, the music grew softer and slower, the champagne flowed as white-jacketed waiters wandered among guests with trays of champagne glasses. Riley watched the guests hit the buffet tables, decorated with ice sculptures shaped like swans and roses, and laden their plates with food from silver chafing dishes. What he never did was let Allie out of his sight.

Dancing with Nick's mother, he maneuvered Teresa toward her son and his new wife. A tap on his shoulder made him laugh; it was Nick's father, cutting in. "Dance with the bride. This one is mine," he said to Riley laughingly.

"No way," Nick replied, holding Ann tightly at the waist. "I'm dancing with my wife." Warmth rushed into Nick's voice. "*Wife*. That word sure sounds great," he murmured, and angled his face to kiss Ann again.

She laughed with him. "It does, doesn't it?"

Riley cleared his throat. "Could you two wait until later?"

"Jealous," Nick gibed back. "Why don't you find your own woman?" he said, not too subtly looking toward Allie.

Away from the crowd, she stood in shadowy darkness. Before meeting her, Riley had never wanted demands on his time, on his life. Mostly he'd never wanted anyone to get too close to him. If he wanted to be fair to her, he would leave her alone now, but he kept walking toward her until he smelled her perfume again.

"It's been a long time, Allie."

At the sound of the familiar voice, Allie turned, sloshing the soda in the glass she held. Deep-set, blue eyes locked with hers as he smiled in that slow, enticing way that had always made her feel wanted.

For a heartbeat, she considered leaving. Only a heartbeat. She wasn't as prone to romantic notions as she'd been two years ago. Since then, she'd accepted that the man she'd once loved had never loved her, that they hadn't been meant for each other. The last night with him at their apartment had put a stop to foolish dreams.

With effort, she produced a smile fit for a toothpaste commercial, even as anxiety tugged at her. "Hi, yourself." She smelled the woodsy scent of his aftershave. What could a woman say to the man who used to kiss her until she was senseless? "You've changed. No beard."

"I'm in homicide now, not vice. You haven't changed. You're as beautiful as ever." It wasn't a line. In bed at night, he used to lose himself in the rich darkness of her eyes while he traced the straightness of her nose, the fullness of her bottom lip; while his fingers moved over her fair skin.

"The bride is," she answered, directing his attention toward the happy couple cutting the cake. "This is pretty impressive," she said in reference to the beautiful estate. "Who would have guessed Nick would marry someone like Gillian Somerset?"

"Ann's not what you might expect," he said, using the name she'd used when she'd had amnesia, a nickname she preferred now.

A safe subject, the bride and groom, Allie decided. "You like her?"

He had from the moment he'd met the classy-looking blonde. "She suits Nick."

"That's an odd thing to say. A cop and a socialite are opposites." So were Riley and she, but they'd lived six months—six wonderful months—together. "How did they meet?"

"She had amnesia when they met."

"Amnesia?"

"It's a long story." A corner of Riley's mouth lifted in a semblance of a grin. "He played hero."

She smiled with him. "Typical of Nick." Riley had once told her that Nick always played the good cop when they were interrogating a suspect.

"Nick met her while he was staying at my cabin." Riley remembered when he'd been with Allie at his Wisconsin cabin. Two weeks alone, fishing, walking in the woods, laughing in the shower, making love in front of the fire. "And Janet? How's she?"

How insane inconsequential talk with him seemed, Allie decided. Once a couple had been intimate, they couldn't go back, couldn't pretend nonchalance. "My mother is busy, as always." Did he feel anything? He was always better than her at hiding emotions.

Others viewed him as laid-back, easy to talk to, quick with laughter. It was part of his masquerade. Only she, because she'd lived with him, had caught glimpses of moodiness, felt that he trapped a myriad

of emotions within him, some too painful to reveal
to anyone.

And that was what had hurt her most. He'd been
caring when she'd broken her arm. He'd been
thoughtful, quick to call if he'd be late coming home.
And he'd been gentle. She would never have fallen
in love with a cold, unresponsive man. But as much
as he'd shared with her, he'd never trusted her
enough, never opened himself completely to her,
never spoke of love.

He laughed suddenly, unexpectedly. "It's weird."

She found herself smiling and didn't know why,
except his smile always had done that to her. "What
is?"

"Trying to play catch-up with someone you know
so well." His grin slipped. "Where did you go after
you left?"

"Go?" The June air seemed suddenly hotter. Raising a hand, she dabbed fingertips at perspiration on
her cheeks and stared at the ice cubes in the glass
she held. She'd like to reach for one and smooth it
over her skin.

"After I got back from Texas, I called your
mother's. For two weeks, all I got was her cheery
message on the answering machine."

"We went to Seattle to visit my aunt." Allie silently groaned at the ridiculously polite conversation.
"I liked it there. I stayed for a while." And she'd
tried to forget him. But she couldn't pretend he was
only a fragment of her past. One little boy made him
a part of every day of her life.

"And you got married." Ridiculous or not, he

couldn't imagine another man knowing her as well as he had.

Allie tensed. He knew! Did he also know about the baby? She didn't think so. Except for a Christmas card, she hadn't had contact with Nick.

"You really meant it when you said you wanted to get married."

How simple he made it sound, but it had been so much more complicated. Emotion constricted her chest like a vice. "Yes, I really meant it." She'd had to think of herself, of the baby—his baby—that she'd carried inside her. So she'd reached for another and had failed. Guilt about Mitch still burdened her. She hadn't deceived him; she'd deceived herself, made herself believe she could forget another man. She'd failed at that, too.

"Nick told me you own an antique store here now."

News traveled quickly on the grapevine. After the wedding ceremony, she'd talked to Nick's sister Mara and had told her about the store.

"What's the name of it?"

"Cherished Treasures."

Riley heard pride in her voice. "You always wanted one. You've done well."

"It was my husband's."

He looked at her left hand, saw the bare ring finger. *Was.* She'd said it *was* her husband's. "Are you divorced?"

"I'm widowed."

He hadn't known. He noted that she said the words smoothly, but he searched for grief behind the darkness of her eyes. He saw none. Though she was delicate looking, he'd always viewed her as a tough lady. What he'd never imagined was her bearing up to the role of a young widow. "I'm sorry." The sympathy was sincere. "Did it happen long ago?"

"No." Allie said no more. Saying too much about Mitch wasn't wise. "Isn't there someone waiting for you?" she asked with a sweep of her hand toward the crowd.

"No, no one."

So he was in between. "They look wonderful together," she said, diverting his attention to Nick and his bride as they danced nearby.

Slowly his gaze moved up from her mouth to meet her stare. Music, soft and dreamy, floated around them. He wanted to dance with her. They'd always danced well together, but if he drew her close, he wasn't sure he'd be able to let her go.

"Where are they going on their honeymoon?"

"A Mediterranean cruise." He couldn't resist. He touched a strand of Allie's hair. It still felt like silk.

Allie didn't pull back, didn't want him to know how vulnerable she still was with him.

"Allison."

It took every effort to look away from the blue eyes she used to drown in. Straight-backed, inching his way around people, Stefan Neubocker appeared annoyed. Allie had never viewed the thin, studious-looking type as white-knight material until that moment.

Riley narrowed his eyes at the impeccably dressed, dark-haired man. Riley had no business wanting her again, but what good sense he had and what he was feeling weren't meshing. He doggedly pursued criminals. He was relentless about seeking answers to questions. At the moment, he wanted to find out where this guy fit in her life. "Who's he?"

"Stefan. Stefan Neubocker." She'd met Stefan months ago at an auction. They'd kept in touch because of a common interest in antiques. Feeling as if she was on a stage, trying not to be aware of an audience, she brushed Stefan's cheek with her own in greeting.

"I had to show every credential in my wallet to get past security," he grumbled as he drew back.

"I'm glad you came," Allie said, to soothe his irritation. Even if he was late, he'd unknowingly arrived just in time.

"I brought this with me," he said, handing her a pamphlet. "I thought you might want to see what Augenheimer is planning to offer at his auction next week."

It wasn't Riley's movement, but Stefan's distracted manner that forced her to make an introduction.

Both men sized each other up.

Behind his wire-rimmed glasses, Stefan's eyes were filled with questions. He knew everything about her marriage to Mitch, about Devin, about Riley.

"Riley?" a woman called.

He slanted a look at the maid of honor, who was gliding toward him.

"The photographer needs us."

He nodded at Sara Vandermein. "Be right there."

Allie was grateful. She opened her purse and dug for her car keys. She didn't want to go on with this. "Nice seeing you again, Riley," she said, managing her best smile. "You must be starving, Stefan." She hooked her arm with his and led him away before he could respond. Tightly she held her keys. Once Stefan had eaten, she would insist that they leave.

Riley watched her until she reached the cobblestone walkway and disappeared around a group of people near the buffet table. Though turning away from her last time hadn't been easy, he'd thought it the best thing he could have done for her. But this wasn't over, he realized.

With another call from Sara, he pivoted toward her. Then he saw the tube of lipstick. Allie might never miss it, but he dropped it into the pocket of his tuxedo jacket, not sure if he was keeping it as a memento of her or as a future excuse to see her again.

Chapter Two

Nearly a week passed. Riley had placed the lipstick tube on his dresser and hadn't touched it again until this morning. Consciously or not, he'd dropped it into his gym bag before driving to the precinct.

Before dawn, he'd wandered into the precinct basement and the weight room. He'd exercised and strained muscles. He'd tried not to think about Allie. No luck. Thoughts so vivid he could remember her taste, smell the sweetness of her, had intruded. He didn't need to be hit with a sledgehammer. She didn't want to see him. He wished he could forget he'd seen her again, but he couldn't.

At the precinct's doorway, he sidestepped two uniformed cops flanking a drunk. Along with two other detectives, he strolled outside to find an overcast sky heavy with pewter gray clouds that promised a summer rain. As he jammed a hand into his pants pocket, paper crinkled. In his mailbox this morning, he'd found a letter from Texas, from his sister. He'd forgotten about it and hadn't read it yet.

For two years, he hadn't heard from her. Whatever his sister wanted to tell him didn't matter. That part of his life was over. She'd said enough. Allie was a different story. She was too near, too tempting for him not to see her again.

Beside him, Joe Morez zipped his duffel bag and raved about his newborn son.

Older and the father of two sets of twins, Bob Dolan boasted about his nine-year-old sons' latest feats on the baseball field. "Amy," he said about his eleven-year-old daughter, "did a back handspring yesterday. She's been interested in gymnastics ever since the Olympics."

Riley let the conversation float over him. He supposed bragging rights about their kids came with fatherhood. He'd never know.

"Was it my imagination or was Allie at Nick's wedding?" Joe asked.

"She was there."

"I'm not big on redheads," Joe said, "but she's what I'd call *extra*ordinary. How did you manage to lose her?"

Bob guffawed. "She wised up. Probably realized if she didn't get out she'd be stuck with him forever," he gibed, motioning with his thumb in Riley's direction. "It was good to see you with her," he said more seriously. "My wife always said that when she was around I heard no one else. Couldn't help myself,'' he said self-deprecatingly. ''She has one of the sexiest laughs.''

Riley didn't need the reminder.

''You playing ball Thursday?'' Joe asked.

With effort, Riley focused on him. ''What?''

''For the lineup. I need to know if you'll be at the field Thursday.''

''I'll be there,'' Riley answered, looking up as a light drizzle began. His car was at the end of the parking lot, the cellular phone in it too far away at the moment. ''See you,'' he said, and about-faced.

''Where are you going?'' Joe asked quizzically.

''To make a phone call.''

Allie awoke to the sound of rain. On a table beside the bed was a digital alarm clock instead of the ballerina music box she'd begged for one Christmas. The room she'd grown up in had changed. A white coverlet had replaced the yellow one. Gone were the posters of rock stars, her shelf of animal knickknacks. An upholstered blue chair angled out from the corner where her desk used to be.

Crowded in another corner where she'd kept a stereo, her son slept in the crib she'd moved with her from the suburban neighborhood that she and Mitch had lived in. She'd sold the house after he'd died and had moved back into her mother's home. Allie had gained nothing from its sale because of a second mortgage. Except for the antique shop, she had only a scraped-together savings account.

While she could have gone into an apartment with Devin, this living arrangement had made more sense.

As her mother had said, she'd have a live-in baby-sitter for when she went out. That wasn't often. There had been a few boys in high school she'd been sweet on, and one man before Riley she'd been infatuated with. Then there had been Mitch. But only one man had ever had her heart. Ironically, Riley was the one who hadn't wanted it.

Padding into the bathroom, she heard the phone ring. Because her mother had received two others in the last fifteen minutes, Allie wondered if her morning plans had disrupted her mother's usual schedule with friends, and if they were busily rearranging their day.

She finished brushing her hair just as she heard Devin stir.

Standing in the crib, he held his arms up to her. He awoke smiling—always. She'd felt blessed that he had such a good disposition. Some single mothers dealt with the strain of a day's work and afterward went home to a cranky child. Allie loved her evenings with him. He laughed easily, enjoying any little game her imagination conceived. He charmed strangers with his quick smiles and friendliness. He was a gift she never felt worthy enough to have.

While she changed his diaper, he stretched his little body, pointing his toes, and smiled at her. Every moment with him was precious to her. Nuzzling his neck, she listened to his giggles and laughed with him, then sat him up to slide a shirt over his head.

"Shews," he said, reaching for his sneaker.

With her head bent close to his, Allie slipped one

sneaker and then the other onto his feet. While she tied the shoes, she laughed as he touched her nose.

"Noz." His little finger moved within the vicinity of her eye. "Eye."

Hugging him, she did a little two-step dance through the hallway. When she reached the kitchen with him in her arms, her mother was setting the telephone receiver back in its cradle. "Are you sure it'll be all right if I take your car?" Allie asked, while pouring cereal in a bowl for Devin.

Yesterday, while driving on the expressway, she'd felt a distinct pull on her steering wheel. With Devin in the back seat, she'd taken no chances and had driven straight to a mechanic. The car would be getting a front-end alignment sometime today, if the mechanic could be believed. She'd have been without a vehicle if her mother hadn't offered her own car.

"I have work to do here, but..." Her mother paused, preoccupied with reaching for cleanser under the sink. As a makeshift safety measure against Devin's curiosity, they'd hooked sturdy rubber bands from one cabinet handle to another. "I was going to suggest you let me drive you to the fitness center this morning," she continued, retrieving the cleanser.

In Seattle, Allie had started exercising regularly. When she'd moved back home, she'd found a fitness center nearby. "That's all right with me." Allie set the bowl on Devin's high-chair tray and lifted him up. In predictable behavior for a sixteen-month-old, he squirmed and verbally protested. To quiet him, she handed him a banana. "I don't open the store until noon today." She preferred starting her workday earlier, but Mitch had liked sleeping in on Monday mornings and had set a late opening time. To cater to regular customers, she'd kept those hours.

Generously, Devin offered her the squashed banana he was holding in his chubby hand. "Thank you," she said, bending over for a pretend bite, then dabbing at the banana on his cheek with a napkin. "When I get home, I'll read your baseball book. Okay?"

"Otay."

Allie kissed his nose. Motherhood hadn't been a part of her goals, but she'd never realized what she would have been missing. Devin was the joy of her life. He was all that mattered now. "Mom, the aerobics class is supposed to be over by ten."

"Then I'll pick you up before eleven," she answered.

That suited Allie. It would give her time to shower. She sipped coffee, expecting, actually waiting, for her mother to ask questions about Riley. Since the wedding, she hadn't said a word about him. That bothered Allie a lot. Such restraint wasn't normal for Janet Harrigan.

"Let me know when you're ready to leave," she said instead, before standing and starting for the door.

"Bye-bye," Devin called out, waving chubby fingers at his grandmother, though she'd be back in a few moments.

Allie smiled. He waved goodbye to everyone and everything, including water fountains, birds and cars.

"Bye, sweetheart."

She's looking too pleased with herself, Allie thought before her mother disappeared from the room. "What's Grandma up to?" she murmured to her son when they were alone.

For the next hour, Allie pushed herself through the class while the lithe instructor breezed through the routine. Advanced aerobics was a killer. As the instructor slowed the pace for a cooling-down stage, Allie ignored aching muscles and the dryness in her mouth. She'd get through this, she thought determinedly.

When the music finally did stop, she bent forward, gasping for breath. Exercising was a love-hate thing. Though she truly detested it, she always felt a triumphant rush afterward.

Dabbing at the perspiration on her face with a small towel, she ambled toward the door. She'd have time for a shower before her mother arrived and would still get to the shop a good hour prior to opening the door for customers.

Showered and dressed within half an hour, she hurried toward the exit. Looking up, she sidestepped a chesty blonde too busy conversing to notice her.

"Now he could warm my bed any day," she said to her companion, with another look back through the glass entrance doors.

As the woman stepped out of Allie's line of vision, she saw Riley lounging against his car. Blue eyes that still heated her blood roamed over her. Her pulse hammering, she raised a hand to brush hair from her face. She wished for a second, just a second, to catch her breath. "I won't ask how you knew where I was," she said with a casualness that cost her dearly. Her mother was running true to form. When the phone had rung earlier, Allie should have grilled her about who had called.

"I learned you were staying at your mother's." He opened the door for her. "She told me you needed a ride this morning."

Allie drew a long, stabilizing breath and settled on the seat. She wanted to beg him to go away before he complicated her life—and Devin's—but she was speechless.

"You dropped this," he said, handing her the lipstick when he slid behind the steering wheel.

So he'd had a reason for coming. "Thanks."

Before turning on the ignition, he rolled down the window. He needed air, something to clear his mind. Desire so strong he'd nearly groaned with it had swept through him when he'd watched her in the class. Her face glowing from the exercise had reminded him of a similar soft, misty sheen clinging to her skin during more intimate moments. He'd known this was a mistake, hadn't he? But he hadn't been able to stop himself from seeing her again. "Want to tell me where I'm supposed to take you?"

Allie rattled off the address for Cherished Treasures. A ride to the store was innocent enough. She'd thank him, they'd say goodbye and that would be the end of it.

Following her directions, Riley drove toward the historic district. "Why are you living with Janet again?" he asked as he eased into traffic.

"It made sense not to keep the house Mitch and I had. I'd just rattle around in it."

Mitch. The husband. Would Riley ever get used to the idea that some other man had been a part of her life?

Allie couldn't stop herself. She had to know. "Are you still living at the apartment?"

"Still there."

The apartment they'd shared had five rooms and a view of the lake. They'd made love on the rug, with the glow of sunrise bathing them. "I'm surprised," she murmured.

He looked puzzled. "Why?"

"Because I always felt it suited me more than you."

He understood her thinking. Before she'd entered his life, he'd been satisfied to call a one-room apartment home. She'd changed his life. He'd known a happiness he'd never expected, then one day nothing was right between them. He knew he hadn't deserved so much happiness. He'd always expected the end to come, but what he'd never understood was why it had happened that day.

Making a final turn, he viewed the abundance of historical cottages, most of them antique shops with quaint names like Lace 'n' Things and Victorian Kingdom. Cherished Treasures stood behind a white picket fence. Potted geraniums lined the stairs; lacy curtains hung in the windows.

Riley parked in front of the store. "Answer one question, will you?" He waited until her eyes met his. "Why? Why all of a sudden did you want marriage?"

Because I was pregnant, scared. "Do you really think it makes sense to…"

"What?" He turned off the ignition and shifted to face her. "Rehash this?" He draped an arm over the steering wheel. "Yeah, I do. I never understood what happened."

Though her parents' separation had soured her feelings about marriage, she'd believed that with Riley she'd found something lasting. "My biological clock was ticking," she said for an excuse that was as close to the truth as possible.

He'd heard of other women worrying about that, but at twenty-seven, she'd had time yet. Something else had to have triggered that turnaround. Maybe if he understood the man she had married, he'd get a handle on why everything between them had gone wrong. "Tell me about your husband. What was he like?"

Allie kept to herself what pained her the most about Mitch. "He was interesting. Intelligent. Handsome." He'd romanced her. They'd met at his store when she'd returned to Chicago with her infant son during a visit to her mother. Allie had been confused by his attentiveness. He'd accepted that another man held her heart. She'd never deceived him. So when she'd returned to Seattle, she'd thought she would never see him again, but he'd followed her. She'd made some poor decisions during the past few years. Marrying Mitch had topped the list. "That time in my life is over."

Riley wanted to ask if she'd married on the rebound, but it was a question he couldn't voice. "Isn't that something people say when that isn't true?"

Being truthful came easier to her than lying. "I'm not mourning, Riley. I did when he died." She'd felt guilty for not giving Mitch what he deserved, then she'd learned he hadn't deserved as much as she'd thought. "But not anymore," she said, opening the door. "Thanks for the ride."

Hunching her shoulders, Allie bowed her head against the slanting rain. At a clipped pace, she dashed toward the store, darting beneath the canopy of one shop before making a final run for her own. She reached the door without getting drenched and fumbled in her purse for her keys.

As she turned the doorknob, Riley slammed a hand on hers to stop her from opening it. He hadn't planned to follow, but he needed an answer. "Why did you marry him?"

Pain begot pain. "Because he loved me enough to ask."

Dark and intense, his eyes probed as if to see inside her. "So it was that easy to walk away from me, to find another?"

No tiptoeing. Allie wasn't surprised. Perhaps this was inevitable. Even after so many years, it was impossible for them to be only friendly acquaintances.

Rain pelted at his back. "Have you changed so much?" he asked, challenging her. "The woman I remember backed away from nothing. She'd have given me an answer."

Allie was stubborn, unbelievably so, growing more

obstinate when faced with barriers. Knuckling under went against every natural tendency she'd developed through childhood. He knew too much about her, knew what buttons to push. But the woman he'd known had changed. She'd become a mother. She wanted to give her son the security she hadn't known as a child. "What's the point in going down memory lane?"

"I want to. Was it easy finding another?" he asked again.

She wanted to hit him. How could he be so indignant when he'd done just that? Pointedly she stared at the hand blocking her. "No, not easy for me. Only for you."

He looked puzzled. "What? What does that mean?"

She owed him no explanations now, but at one time she'd had no secrets from him. "I'd like to go in."

Standing in the rain made no sense to him, either. He opened the door and followed her in. Before he left her, he'd get an answer to that question.

Allie steadied herself, remembering that in minutes her assistant would arrive. Maybe even a customer. She'd be safe then from her own susceptibility to him.

Stepping farther in, he stood near a Governor Winthrop desk and ran a hand over his damp face. Let him browse. With loving care, she cradled a porcelain ballerina and set it in a box filled with tissue. If she kept busy, he'd get bored and eventually leave.

Interested, Riley eyed the two front rooms, separated by an archway. Garage-sale junk cluttered one. A table held an odd assortment of cheap porcelain figurines; a far corner was filled with antique-looking farm implements; a display case revealed gaudy-looking costume jewelry.

In the other room, dozens of chandeliers show-cased expensive old furniture arranged in room displays. The finest crystal and china and delicate linens showed off highly polished dining room tables. Behind glass cabinet doors, more crystal, including some oddly shaped bowls, sparkled.

Too much rivaled for attention, from mirrors with gilt edges to ornately carved cabinets and glass cases filled with crystal and porcelain figures of dancers and vases. Even spittoons had had class in ages past. He pivoted away from a porcelain one to wander the other rooms, but suddenly froze. Filtered light from a stained-glass window flamed Allie's hair and shadowed her pale skin with the lacy design of its border. She still tied his guts in knots without doing anything. "I like the store."

Bent over, Allie reached for a tissue in her shoulder bag tucked under the counter. She didn't answer.

"This is nice."

She heard his appreciative tone, and straightening, saw him touching a mahogany bureau she'd fallen in love with at first sight. She could already see it against one particular wall in her mother's home.

"Are you going to sell this?"

"Not if I can help it."

"What's this?"

"A chamber pot."

Grimacing, he set it down and brushed his hand on a denim-clad thigh. "Who'd want one?"

At his gesture, Allie stifled a grin. If he started amusing her again, she'd lose all resistance. "The historical society." She finished taping a box for shipment, then rounded the counter to set an enormous, pink pig cookie jar closer to salt and pepper shakers. "They need authentic pieces to furnish the homes in the historic district." Allie looked back in response to the jingling of the bell above the door.

Shaking her umbrella outside, her assistant mumbled something under her breath before stepping in and closing the door. Petite, with brown curly hair and deep-cut dimples, Carol Tumpton was a divorced mother of two who looked far younger than thirty-three. "What a rain. It's…" Her voice trailed off. Her dark eyes, suddenly glued on Riley, sparkled with curiosity.

As Allie made an introduction, Carol beamed with approval.

And Mr. Charm wasn't helping. He flashed Carol a smile guaranteed to trip any female heartbeat. Allie decided to take control. "Carol, could you help that customer by the medieval weapons?"

"I've got him," she said eagerly, giving Allie a knowing wink when her back was to Riley.

Silently Allie groaned. Between her mother and Carol, she was sandwiched by incurable romantics.

"What's this?" Riley asked again, stumped as he examined a worn-looking wood table holding some kind of farm machinery with a crank and gear.

Allie felt as if she was waiting for the other shoe

to drop. "That's a pea huller. It was patented between 1899 and 1903." Not looking at him, she took off toward the back of the historic cottage. "Carol will answer any questions you have, Riley. I have paperwork to do."

With that dismissal, she wandered through smaller rooms—a Victorian bedroom exhibiting hand-laced linens, a parlor featuring Chippendale chairs and Sheraton tables, and another room cluttered with Victorian pieces, including children's toys. Each of the eight rooms was uniquely decorated, except the oversize pantry and enclosed back porch, which she used for storage. Still in its original state was the cottage's kitchen. With a desk shoved in a far corner, it served as an office and a break room for her and Carol.

Not following her had never entered Riley's mind. "Tell me now."

With a gasp, she swung around. Why had she thought he'd let her dismiss him so easily?

"What the hell were you talking about before?" he asked, noting the mound of paperwork on the desk. "I never cheated on you."

To calm her nerves, she moved to the coffee brewer. "No, but it didn't take you long to forget me."

How wrong she was. "I'd say that was mutual." He studied her closely, wishing he could see inside her mind. Marriage. Kids. Why had she wanted that so badly, so suddenly? "Why don't we just clear the air?" he asked, stepping behind her.

"Clear the air about what?"

He noticed her hand wasn't quite steady as she poured coffee into two cups. "You're angry at me."

"No, I'm not."

"Yeah, you are," he insisted. Rightfully so, he thought. She shouldn't trust him, shouldn't even want to talk to him. But that wasn't her way. And he'd take advantage of her as he had before.

Her own pride balked at discussing what had been painful for her. "I called you," she blurted out, turning to face him squarely.

He looked bewildered. "You called me?"

Allie couldn't dodge the anger resurfacing in her. That phone call had sealed the fate of three lives. Guilt heavy within her, she'd believed she had to tell him the truth about Devin. What he would say, what he might feel hadn't mattered at that moment. Every second of every day she was away from him she'd agonized with her guilt about keeping Devin a secret from him.

"When?" He drilled a hard, questioning look at her. "When did you call?"

Allie wished she'd never mentioned it, but she wanted to defend herself, to make him aware she hadn't left him and waltzed swiftly into another man's arms. "A month after I left, I came back. That's when I called you."

"You called, but you didn't leave a message on the answering machine?" he asked, as if trying to clarify her action in his mind.

"There was no need." Accusation colored her tone. "I talked to someone."

"Talked to who? Nick?" No one else who'd ever

been in his apartment would have picked up his phone.

"A woman." With that one phone call, Allie had forced herself to face a fact. He'd gone on with his life.

Riley mulled over her words. During the past two years, he'd dated women, but he'd spent nights at their homes, not his. No woman had stepped foot into his apartment since Allie had left him. And during that first month alone, he'd had no desire to seek out any other woman. What woman could have...? He grimaced as his mind wandered back to those days. One woman *had* been in his apartment, though not by his choice. "What did she say to you?"

"She was..." Oh, what was the point in discussing this now?

"What? Lay an explanation on me."

Not prone to jumping to conclusions, at first Allie had clung to the telephone receiver and the rational thought that the woman was his sister. "Possessive."

Patience came with police work. He'd learned to take his time with interrogations, to draw out answers. He felt as if he'd met a worthy opponent this time. "Allie, just tell me what she said."

The last thing she wanted to do was discuss some other woman. "What does it matter?"

The need for answers drove him every day of his life at work. No way would he let the conversation end with questions still in his mind. As she shifted to move away, he caught her arm, halting her. "It matters to me," he said in a low voice. "Tell me."

The fingers curled over her arm held her firmly.

"I asked to talk to you. She said that you were busy." Because that sounded lame even to her own ears, Allie tried to explain. "She said it in the way a woman conveys 'hands off, he's mine.' But I left a message asking you to call me at my mother's. You never did." When he hadn't, she'd made another decision. If Riley had forgotten her so easily, she'd forget him. A prideful reaction, one that eventually had made her turn to another man.

Under his breath, Riley muttered an earthy curse. If he was calculating this right, she'd called when his apartment had been used as a safe house. "She was in protective custody."

"What?" Allie rounded on him with a doubting look. She'd never heard of the police using one of their detective's apartments to shelter a witness. "You allowed a witness in protective custody to answer the phone?" she questioned, skeptical about such a possibility.

"Allowed?" Riley released a mirthless laugh. "This one did what she wanted. She hated being in police custody. A hooker. She did everything she could to make us all miserable, because she wanted to be out of there. We had her at a hotel, and she called her pimp. So we had to move her quickly. I drew the unlucky straw."

Allie took in a hard breath, aware what his words really meant. A stupid twist of fate had kept her from talking to him.

"While she was at my place, she was just as uncooperative. I can only assume she thought it was a great joke to screw up my personal life by telling you that.''

Confused, Allie turned her back. She needed to be alone, to think. All she'd believed about Riley since leaving him had been wrong. There hadn't been another woman so soon after she'd left. If she'd known the truth, if she'd told him she was pregnant, how different would their lives be now?

Too vulnerable. She had always been too vulnerable around him. ''That was then,'' she said quietly. She was accountable for more than herself now, she made herself remember. One little boy relied on her to make sound decisions.

That was then, he mused, as she hurried toward the main part of the shop to answer the ringing phone. She was right. Yesterdays meant nothing. They couldn't be changed.

Chapter Three

Scrambling for control, Allie stepped behind the counter and struggled to focus on Stefan's words.

"So I'll see you this evening at seven?" he asked.

She managed some coherence. "Seven is fine, Stefan."

As she set down the receiver, she looked up and found herself staring into Riley's eyes.

With great restraint, he'd kept silent about Neubocker until now. "You're going out with Neubocker again?"

"A business date," Allie answered, rounding the counter to nudge a Duncan Phyfe chair closer to a wall.

Right! The guy probably had one thing on his mind—her. Riley frowned at her averted face, wishing he could see her eyes. "Where are you going?"

"Stefan was invited to a cocktail party. He's interested in purchasing some antiques from the host's estate."

Having some other guy romancing her gnawed at him. Hell, there had been a husband. Some other man had seen her sleepy eyed in the morning, had smelled the freshness of lemon in her shampooed hair, had tasted every inch of her skin, too. Riley had no claim on her, he struggled to remember. "Are you wearing the same dress you wore to the wedding?"

"I might."

Another look at her in that dress, at those legs, and only if ice ran through Neubocker's veins would he think about business. "So Neumocker is what?"

"Neubocker," she corrected. Riley was not as dense as he was pretending.

"Whatever." He watched her delicate fingers graze a rolltop desk almost like a caress. He knew that touch, had shuddered beneath it. "What is he?"

"What is he?" Allie bit back a smile. "You make that sound as if I have a choice between human and alien."

He scowled at her. "Don't be cute. You know what I meant. What is he to you?" Riley insisted. "Is he only an acquaintance? Or is he…?"

"He's a museum curator."

"Meaning what?" he asked, impatient with her stingy responses. "You have a lot in common?"

Allie wondered why she even had to explain. What was happening in her life was none of his business. "He's not like you," she answered, returning to the counter.

Riley sidled close to her at the counter and leaned a hip against it. "Should I be insulted?"

"He's dependable."

"You mean boring?"

"Predictable."

"You mean he doesn't want to run out for tacos at three in the morning?"

A sweet memory sprang to her mind. They'd dashed through rain and had sat until dawn in that fast-food restaurant, talking, holding hands. When the sun had appeared, they'd gone home and made love again. "I've never been with him at three in the morning."

The gleam in Riley's eyes was purely masculine. "That's reassuring."

She felt a tug at her heart. If only he would stop grinning at her like that.

"Allie?" Carol looked apologetic for intruding. "There's another phone call for you," she said, beaming a smile in Riley's direction.

Whoever the caller was had perfect timing. "Thank you, Carol." Allie definitely needed time and distance from Riley. Her optimism was short-lived.

"I want to talk to you," the caller demanded instead of offering a greeting.

Instinctively Allie tensed at the sound of her brother-in-law's voice. Jason hadn't spoken to her since Mitch's funeral. From past experience with Mitch's older brother, she assumed this call meant one thing—trouble.

"I'm coming over," Jason announced brusquely.

Allie nibbled her bottom lip. This wouldn't do. If Jason came with some problem, Riley wouldn't leave. The last thing she needed was him involved in her life. "I won't be here, Jason."

"Be there," he demanded with his usual arrogance.

She sneaked a look at Riley. As if holding something foreign, he was rotating in his hand an ornate doorstop shaped like a teapot. Like bloodhounds, did cops instinctively smell trouble before it existed? Getting a grip on the uneasiness fluttering within her, she took her time setting the receiver back in its cradle. Whatever Jason wanted, she'd deal with it later. Right now she had a more immediate problem.

Smile. Smile and act normal, she told herself. Riley could always read her too easily. "Want to go to lunch?"

"Lunch?"

A skeptical look narrowed his eyes. The invitation had come too quickly and too soon after the phone call, Allie knew. Well, she couldn't retract it now. Let his suspicions flourish. "What do you say?"

Riley wanted to know who Jason was. He felt irritated that she suddenly had so many men in her life. "Sure."

"Let's go somewhere close." Allie snatched her shoulder bag from under the counter. "I'll be back shortly, Carol." She glanced at the clock before preceding Riley outside. She decided the best defense might be an offensive move. She'd keep moments together pleasant, but not too pleasant.

In his car, she directed him away from the historic

cottages and the cobblestone walkway and old lamp-posts, to one lined with industrial buildings and car-repair shops. With searching eyes, she spotted what looked like a garage stuck between a muffler-repair shop and an empty lot. She would stay away for half an hour, then return alone. By then, Jason should have arrived. "What about there?"

She'd pointed to what looked to Riley like a biker's hangout. "Got a craving for grease?" he queried, as he pulled over and parked.

"Do you think that's the house specialty?" Against her will, her heart tugged at the crooked grin he sent her.

"Salmonella."

Allie nearly giggled as she climbed out of the car. That wasn't wise, either. She couldn't afford to be amused. "You still see the worst in every situation first," she said, more critically than she intended.

He took no offense. Instead he laughed at himself. "I'm a cop." Slipping an arm under her elbow, Riley hustled her toward the door. He viewed this lunch as a diversion. Something was going on in her life. Something that had nothing to do with him, but made her nervous as hell. *None of your business,* he reminded himself. She had her life; he had his. The rationalizing didn't help, since he couldn't seem to switch off his feelings for her.

One step in, Allie decided that he'd evaluated the restaurant accurately. The smells of grease and to-bacco hung in the air. Music blasted from a jukebox. Bikers sat on stools at the counter and crowded booths near the pool table. At a corner booth, a road crew flirted with a waitress.

Riley eyed one girl with purple hair and a ring in her nose who was scoffing down pancakes like she hadn't eaten in weeks. Placing his hand at the small of Allie's back, he ushered her around a pool table and a three-hundred-pound tattooed giant who smelled worse than a skunk.

"What will you have?" the waitress asked even before they'd sat. She looked bored with the world.

Riley ordered coffee for both of them, then hunched forward with a warning. "Keep your jacket on."

Allie's fingers stilled. Beneath the hunter green jacket, she wore a white, T-shirt-style blouse. "Why?"

"Do what you're told."

She arched a haughty brow. "I believe that attitude went out with the—"

"Never mind," he said irritably.

"What is your problem?"

"Every guy in this place is panting over you."

She couldn't help it; her face lit with a smile at his exaggeration. "That's very flattering."

Eyes narrowed, he sent a warning look at one guy ogling her legs. "What is?"

"That you think they are."

"No. Every guy is." A muscle twitched in his jaw. "What do you want to eat?"

She thought he was grinding his teeth. "They won't mess with us."

"And how did you come to that conclusion?"

"You're a cop," she said matter-of-factly.

"Since it's not tattooed on my forehead, how would they know?"

"They don't." Enjoying herself more than she should have, she avoided his stare and perused the grease-stained menu. "I do. So I feel safe." Too many commendations for bravery, for duty above and beyond were stuffed in his bottom dresser drawer for her not to know the courage he possessed.

Keeping an eye on the local talent, he didn't bother to glance at the menu. "Tell me about the store," he urged, though he was more interested in knowing about the phone call she'd received.

Allie lowered the menu to stare out the rain-streaked window at cars passing by. "What about it?"

"Your husband started it?" he asked, noting a definite tilt of her head and her preoccupation with his watch. "It's five minutes later than it was when we left your store."

Allie lifted her head and laughed. "Why would I want to know that?"

That was what he wanted to find out.

"Actually, Mitch's parents owned the shop," she said, to sidetrack him. "This one and two others. When Mitch and Jason, his brother, took over the stores," Allie continued, "Mitch took the one I have, and Jason took the one in an upscale section of Chicago. Then they divided all the inventory from the third shop and closed it." She fell silent, watching the waitress approach their table.

She reminded Allie of a gum-chewing caricature

with mile-high hair, from an old-time television sit-com about waitresses. "You want anything else?" she asked, while setting two cups of coffee on the table.

With the natives so restless, Riley decided that a quick exit made sense. "Hamburgers to go."

That wasn't what Allie had planned, but she couldn't help feeling smug. Obviously her restaurant choice had prevented a leisurely meal. If she played it smart, she'd be okay. "Do you want to eat in the car?"

"We'll take the food back to your store." He reached for his wallet. "You mentioned Jason? He's the one who upset you?"

Of all the traits that she wished she could change, her inability to hide her emotions ranked as first on her list. "He doesn't like me."

Riley had never met anyone who didn't like Allie. Outgoing, friendly, she made people feel at ease instantly. All his adult life he'd been a loner, until he'd met her. She'd been the only person he'd willingly invited into his life.

"He made it clear when Mitch and I married that he thought his brother had made a mistake," she said, standing with him as the waitress brought their food, already bagged, to them.

"Let's go." He slid a hand under her elbow and snatched up the bag.

She noticed he hadn't sampled even one sip of the coffee. "You really don't like that place, do you?" she asked as he ushered her out of the diner.

"You've chosen better."

More roughly than usual, he gripped her arm and propelled her out from under the diner's canopy.

The french fry she was fishing out of the bag flew from her fingers at the abrupt movement. "Will you stop playing Neanderthal man?"

"Get in the car." He swiveled and glanced back. They had company. Three bikers had wandered outside, eyes still riveted on her. Riley flung open the door on the passenger's side. Alone, he'd have planted his feet and stared them down.

"Riley—"

"In," he insisted, with a look over the car's roof. Company was closing in on them. "Defending your honor against half a dozen sex-crazed—"

"Sex-crazed?" With a laugh, Allie followed his stare to the tattooed, bearded threesome. "Oh." Without another word, she scrambled into the vehicle.

"When did you become so foolhardy?" he grumbled when they were in traffic again.

"When did you get so—so…"

He slanted a look at her. His squint in place, he warned, "Be careful."

Allie smothered a giggle and chose silence. How easy it would be to forget all that had gone wrong between them, she realized. She nibbled on a french fry while he drove back to her store. Since he planned on eating there, she'd have to talk to Jason in the main part of the store. She hoped that he would keep his voice low for a change.

With no umbrella, she dashed with Riley from one

storefront overhang to the next. With luck, she'd get him to the back of the store before Jason arrived.

No luck was needed.

"Jason came and left," Carol announced when they stepped inside. "Breezed in and breezed out," she murmured, not veiling her dislike for the man. "Too busy to waste more time waiting for you. That's what he said."

"Was he angry?"

"He came in angry, Allie. He's always angry."

Whatever his reason for this impromptu visit, Allie sensed he'd play havoc with her life.

Curiosity in full gear, Riley trailed her to the kitchen at the rear of the store. "What did the brother-in-law say to you on the phone that has you on edge?"

Allie forged ahead with an explanation designed to stop his questions. "Because we lived in Seattle for a while, Mitch wasn't here like he should have been to deal with business. Jason called to tell me that I should thank him for keeping the store going." What else he wanted was what really worried her.

Riley settled a hip on the edge of the desk and touched the leaf of a plant on the corner of it. Like her mother, she had a green thumb, had nurtured an apartment full of plants. "Gracious man," he returned snidely.

Allie noticed the philodendron needed water. "I do appreciate what he did," she said honestly and dug in the grease-stained bag for a hamburger. "Mitch stayed in Seattle longer than he should have."

It took no effort to guess why. "Because of you?" Riley asked, accepting the hamburger from her.

Allie knew that was true, and felt badly. If Mitch had left, then what had happened... She stopped the thought. She wasn't sure what had motivated Mitch toward the trouble he'd gotten into during the last months before he died. "After he died, I wasn't thinking about the business, so Jason handled the store for a few more weeks."

Perched on the edge of her desk, Riley dropped the hamburger back in the bag. "It's not easy for a man to let you go." He smiled a little at the surprise he saw in her eyes. "I couldn't," he said softly, good sense forgotten. With a featherlight touch, he brushed his thumb across her cheek. "You know, the first time I saw your face I wanted to memorize it."

Sensation slithered through her from his caress. She didn't want him touching her. She didn't want to reminisce. There was so much that had never been said. And what he needed to hear couldn't be said now, here.

"Remember that day?"

She did, as if it was yesterday. Unlike today, with the warmth of a June breeze barely fluttering leaves, and the activity of the city around them, it had been a cooler autumn day when they'd met—in the local forest preserve during a law-enforcement picnic. Neighbors—a policeman and his wife—had invited her.

"An eye-stopping redhead in cut-off shorts hit a grounder to me at third base." He'd been sunk from that moment. He'd had his share of women—enough to know this one was different from others. He'd thrown the ball—too slowly, because he'd been watching her run, staring at those long, tanned legs. He'd missed the next fly ball. The outfielder had caught it. Like a kid waiting for Santa Claus, Riley had anticipated the moment when the next batter would connect with the ball, when she'd come running from second to third base toward him. But the next two batters had struck out, and with a laugh, she'd jogged back to the bleachers instead of to him. "I spent the game watching you," he confessed.

Allie looked down. There was so much danger in remembering. Danger in being this close. Even the sight of his hands roused a remembrance of loving, of hands so gentle that she'd sighed beneath their caresses, so demanding she'd moaned from their magic.

"I sat through a lunch of hot dogs and potato salad, watching you." He'd bowed out of playing a volleyball game to watch her. He'd listened to her laugh, a soft, husky sound that had enticed him. Now, as her fragrance teased him, he thought of all the times he'd watched her dab perfume at her throat, all the times he'd drawn in that scent when his mouth had pressed against her flesh.

Her pulse throbbing, Allie couldn't look away from his eyes. She felt the pull—intense, insistent. "I remember, but we weren't right for each other," she said, drawing back to escape his touch. Another second and she'd have stepped into his arms; she'd have kissed him. "I did want more than you did."

She was wrong. But he'd never tell her that. Sometimes he'd thought he would die inside whenever a memory of her returned. And there had been many. How often had she snuggled against him in the darkness of their bedroom while he listened to her laugh through reruns of *I Love Lucy* or cry during Hallmark card commercials? She'd been his friend and his lover. "We enjoyed the time we did have together."

She'd never forget a moment of it.

"I made your heart quicken." His suddenly soft, sensuous tone jolted her heart. "You made my blood boil."

He wanted her. As schooled as he was to restrain reactions, block emotions, with her, he couldn't deny that he always felt as if he was a breath away from losing all control.

"I'm different, Riley."

"So you don't feel anything for me anymore?"

She started to look away, because to stare into his eyes only weakened her more. He caught her chin. As his gaze drifted down to linger on her mouth, all the excitement and heat were with her again. "I won't pretend I'm not still attracted to you." What she felt for him was unimportant. In the end, he wouldn't give Devin what he really needed. Who knew better than her the harm a part-time father caused?

"I want to be friends," she managed to say calmly. Anger between them would have been easier on her. But he was Devin's father. An amiable relationship between them was vital. She didn't want them sniping at each other. No one gained anything then, and one person lost—the child. No, she wouldn't put Devin in the middle just because they lacked the maturity to get along. "I mean that. I do want to be friends."

Idly, his gaze roamed over her face. He wanted to drag her against him. "That works for me."

Allie straightened her back, wary at his quick agreeableness. As he crowded her, she placed a hand on his chest to keep him from drawing her against him. In his arms, she would battle every memory they'd shared, every dream she'd imagined since they'd separated. "Any other involvement makes no sense."

"You're right," he said, lightly toying with strands of her hair. Silky, they fell over his fingers as if caressing them. He knew better than to push this. He was no good for her, yet he found himself wanting the closeness like before. Bending his head, he brushed his lips across hers. "You don't need this." He felt her catch her breath. "I don't, either." But this wasn't about need. His fingers grazed her jaw. Want. It was about want. "That doesn't mean I don't want you," he whispered against her warm, soft mouth. As he sampled the sweetness that he'd been addicted to years ago, he felt the craving for her intensifying.

"It's too late." She didn't want this. It was insane. Just being with him unlocked too much hurt. They couldn't be lovers again.

"Maybe it is," he said, making himself turn away from her.

Outside, he swore at himself, at her, at what had been lost. For months after she'd left, he'd convinced himself that he'd forgotten her. Of course, he'd been lying. Being so near her now, he hungered for her again. Nothing surpassed an afternoon in bed with sunlight and desire warming them. How often had he longed for the sound of her voice, yearned for the smoky laughter that sprang from her unexpectedly?

God, he still needed her. After all this time, she reached inside him like no woman ever had. Only she had ever touched him. Only she had made him feel whole. And scared.

Chapter Four

Emotions too strong to resist had pulled at Allie. Just the brush of his mouth, the heat of it, had bathed her in a shower of confusion.

For a long while after he left, she was still waiting for tension to ease away. To be with him again meant risking her heart. It meant bringing him into Devin's life. But for how long would he stay?

Unconsciously she straightened her shoulders. Be strong. Be firm. She had to keep a clear head and not let emotion guide her.

What was between them was over.

During the rest of the afternoon, she sat at the desk with her eyes glued to the computer monitor to keep her mind on business. One fact was obvious—she should have gotten more involved in the finances of the shop. But aware of Jason's attitude toward her, she'd never pushed Mitch to share that information with her. She'd assumed the business, in a good location and with a good reputation for fairness, was doing well. It would have been if it weren't for a handful of unpaid bills. Running her fingers over her tired eyes, she finally pushed away from the desk, to see Carol in the doorway.

"I thought you might want part of my dinner," she said, holding up a submarine sandwich.

Allie shook her head. "Thanks, no, but I'll take part of your orange." The only downside to being a boss was moments like this. *Carol, I'm not sure how long you'll have your job.* A soft heart made it difficult for Allie to say those words.

"You've been in here for hours." Carol handed her the orange. "Is the shop in financial trouble?"

If she was discriminating in making purchases, if she found buyers for some of the more valuable inventory, she might clear those bills, keep the shop running, keep Carol and herself employed. "No, nothing is wrong."

"Good." Carol poured more coffee into her cup. "If I needed a job, I doubt Jason would hire me. I don't bow well."

Allie hunched over her desk to peel the orange.

"I thought it was great when you took over the store. I knew Mitch wasn't really interested in it."

"No, I don't think he was," Allie agreed. While she loved the store, Mitch had merely fallen into the trap of doing what was expected of him. She smiled at Carol and led her into conversation about Mrs. Isley Manford, one of their best customers.

Somehow, Allie vowed that she'd keep the shop going. She'd lost one dream already. She wouldn't lose another.

Several hours later, feeling grimy from pushing around cartons in the storeroom, Allie found herself caught in a traffic jam on her way home. Impatiently she tapped her fingertips on the steering wheel and gave up her hope for a lengthy shower before Stefan arrived.

Instead, she managed half an hour with Devin and a short shower. Shimmying into her dress, she considered pinning her hair up while she contorted to reach back for the zipper. She snagged the little clip as her mother stepped behind her to take over the task. "Thank you," Allie said.

"What time is Stefan picking you up?"

Allie strolled to the dresser for a brush. "He should be here in fifteen minutes."

Stretched out in his crib, arms up over his head, Devin slept peacefully.

Her mother's expression grew solemn. "I know you. You've smiled and laughed since you've come home, but you're worried about something."

Allie exhaled deeply. Was she so obvious? "Jason," she said, because he, like Riley, had become a problem.

Annoyance slipped into her mother's voice after Allie told her about the phone call. "Do you have any idea what he wants?"

Allie responded with a shake of her head.

Her mother released an unladylike snort. "You

went through a great deal with his brother. I suppose he doesn't think about that.''

Allie had kept no score sheet, but she had been the one Carol had called and consulted with to make decisions about the shop when Mitch had shown no interest in the business.

''No woman Mitch ever brought home would have pleased Jason,'' her mother commented, while dropping some of Devin's toys in the laundry basket, a makeshift toy box.

Allie believed she was right, but one fact remained. In Jason's eyes, a woman with a child had tricked his brother into marriage.

''Stefan must be here.''

She snapped herself out of her reverie to see her mother heading for the door. As the doorbell rang, obviously not for the first time, Allie pivoted toward the closet. ''I'll be right out,'' she said, and wiggled her foot into a pump. The other one she finally found crammed behind several shoe boxes.

''It wasn't Stefan.''

On her knees, Allie glanced over her shoulder.

Her mother stood in the doorway with a florist box cradled in her arms. ''I wonder if they're roses.''

Allie could have ignored roses. Her breathing deepened with excitement while she opened the box and smelled the scent of lily of the valley and her favorite flowers. Nestled amid leaves of green tissue in the florist's box was a bouquet of white daisies and one vivid, brilliant blue iris.

''Pretty.'' Beside her, her mother sniffed exaggeratingly. "And unusual. Those aren't from Stefan, are they?"

She knew darn well they weren't.

"He hardly seems the type to send flowers."

Her mother had assessed Stefan accurately. To his heart's desire, Rebecca—who was on a scientific expedition in South America—he'd sent a box of *National Geographic* magazines, a sensible gift that lasted. "Of course he didn't send them." Allie made herself reach for the card still in the envelope.

Just because.

Riley.

He knew her soft spots. She'd always been a sucker for flowers. And he'd always been generous in buying them for her. No reason. Just because she loved them.

Allie looked up to find her mother peering over her shoulder to read the card. She didn't even bother to veil her pleased smile. "I'll get a vase," she offered.

Allie expected another unnecessary comment about Riley being so perfect for her.

"Allie?"

Here it comes, she mused.

"I'd better confess," her mother said, pausing in the doorway.

"Confess?" Allie asked warily.

"Early this morning I invited Riley to the barbecue tomorrow evening."

Oh, Mother, what have you done? "Why?"

"I wanted to see him again." Her face mirrored Allie's frown. "You're upset with me?"

Allie wished she was. What she felt bothered her more: her heart was beating too fast with what she recognized as excitement. "Did he say he was coming?"

"He said that he'd try."

Allie gave her head a shake. So he still sat on the fence whenever he felt any kind of pressure. "Mom, his coming here won't make a difference."

"He'll see Devin."

Yes, that's what Allie assumed had been her reason for inviting him. She sighed with exasperation at her mother's persistence. Allie had thought an earlier scolding about her mother sending him to pick her up at the fitness center would have been sufficient. "His knowing that I was pregnant wouldn't have made a difference, Mom." And she wouldn't have wanted it to. She hadn't wanted marriage with him because he'd felt some sense of duty to her and Devin. "He carries a lot of emotional baggage from when his parents died. He had a younger brother and sister to care for. At sixteen," she added, "that's a lot to ask of someone. It made him, for some reason, not want to commit to anyone."

"How did he do that?" her mother asked. "Take care of them?"

Allie shrugged. He'd never told her. She'd always wondered what secrets Riley harbored that were so bad he couldn't share them with her. She'd believed when you loved someone you trusted that other person enough to share everything. He never had. Pregnancy had forced her to wake up to that fact. She'd fallen in love with him. She'd carried his baby, but though she believed he truly cared about her, and knew that he desired her, never had he uttered the word *love*. "Expect him to leave as soon as he's done eating."

"I have more faith in him."

"He doesn't even know I have a child, Mom."

From behind her, she heard her mother's quiet, "Oh."

Unable to resist, Allie sniffed the flowers again, then handed the box to her mother. She supposed she'd have to call and thank him for them. She dropped her shoe and reached for the telephone, then punched out his phone number.

It rang three times before he offered a greeting.

"Riley, it's me." For a long moment he was quiet, so quiet that she wondered if she'd have to say her name.

"Hi."

Allie coiled the telephone cord around a finger. She'd expected the surprise she heard in his voice. What she wasn't prepared for was the purr of pleasure. "The flowers came." Ridiculously, she felt as nervous as a sixteen-year-old calling for a first date. "Thank you."

"You're welcome."

"Why did you send them?"

He caught the tightness in her voice, imagined that telephone cord coiled around one of her fingers by now. Since leaving her, he'd had only a few moments when he hadn't thought of her. "You always liked them."

Allie hesitated, not as sure of herself now as she'd

been when she'd punched out his number. "Mom said she invited you to her barbecue tomorrow evening. Are you coming?"

He swept a glance around his living room. It needed cleaning, the dust on his coffee table so thick he could write his name in it.

Yes or no? she nearly yelled because of his silence.

"I'll be there." He knew that what he was doing was dumb. He'd broken off with her before to save her from the biggest mistake in her life—more involvement with him. And in time, he knew he would push her away again, because he had to. But there was a difference this time. He'd reasoned that she'd done the marriage bit already. He had no idea if it had been a good marriage or not, but he doubted she wanted another emotional involvement so soon. "Are you still going out with Neubocker this evening?"

"He should be here any minute."

Because she was quiet, Riley choked out appropriate words. "Have a good time."

"Thanks. See you." With a sigh, Allie set down the receiver, then collapsed against the wall, nerves already fluttering in her stomach.

"Allie..." Her mother hesitated, as if she was forming words carefully in her mind. "Be fair to him."

Moving away from the mirror, Allie stepped closer to the crib. Because it calmed her, she ran a soothing hand over her sleeping son's fair hair. *He never said he loved me, Mom.* "I can't let him into our lives."

That wasn't what she meant. He wouldn't let her in. Not like he should, and anything less wouldn't be enough.

She looked back as her mother fiddled unnecessarily with the bouquet in a vase. What wasn't she saying? Allie didn't have to wait long to find out.

"It's possible Riley might see himself in Devin, Allie."

Whenever Allie had imagined the moment of them meeting, she'd doubted Riley would see what seemed so obvious to her. Devin had her coloring, but his small face bore Riley's strong features and square jaw. Every time she looked at Devin, she saw his father. "He won't, because he wouldn't want to."

She wondered often what she would tell Devin about his father. Too soon he would start asking questions. She couldn't lie to him and pretend that Mitch was his father. It wouldn't be fair to Devin. He deserved to know who his father was. He needed to know how much she'd loved him.

What if she told Riley and he was pleased? What if he wanted a family now? Wasn't that pure fantasy? The kind of a life he'd chosen was the one he wanted. In fact, it occurred to her that when he learned she had a child, he might back away. That would be proof how wrong they really were for each other, wouldn't it?

By the next afternoon, Allie hadn't shaken off her uncertainties about Riley seeing Devin. Running late because of a customer's indecisiveness about a purchase, she rushed into the bedroom and quickly changed into shorts, a T-shirt and sandals. Since a neighbor's teenage daughter had shown up early, Allie ushered Devin outside to the backyard and left him in her capable care.

A step from the kitchen doorway, her stride faltered as she caught sight of her mother hugging Riley.

"You, lady, still warm my heart," he said warmly.

"Oh, such blarney," she returned with a laugh. As expected, her mother proved as much of a sucker for his smile as she had been before. "He came to help," she said, noticing Allie now. "Wasn't that nice?"

"Nice." Allie jammed a hand in a pocket of her shorts. He'd done that often enough. In fact, he'd do anything asked of him. He'd cooked, cleaned. He'd been a perfect roommate. And lover.

This wouldn't be easy, she mused. At this moment, seeing him here in her mother's sunny kitchen, she wanted to remember only the good times. Such foolishness would haunt her, she knew. They were wrong for each other now.

With her usual enthusiasm, her mother swept them into her preparations for the barbecue. While Riley washed his hands at the kitchen sink, Allie began peeling shells from hard-boiled eggs. Twenty of them.

"I'll give you my recipe for the deviled eggs. Will you mash the yolks for me?"

Nodding, Allie peripherally caught Riley's grin at the task she'd been given.

"Riley, you can mix this," her mother said in regard to a bowl of potato salad.

This was definitely too cozy, too familiar, Allie decided, recalling all the other times they'd divided cooking chores before one of her mother's parties. "How many people did you invite?"

Busy wrapping cobs of corn in aluminum foil, she answered without looking up. "Eighteen. You know most of them." She rattled off the names of several neighbors. "There's also Professor Rowdy."

Allie smiled at the name and strolled to the doorway to peek at Devin, who was hitting a golf ball around. Behind her, Allie caught the buzz of whispers. When she glanced back, her mother gave her a look of innocence personified and quickly moved away from Riley to mold the plastic wrap over the rim of the bowl containing potato salad.

"The professor is a bit eccentric," she continued, "but he's a neighbor's brother."

Riley stifled a laugh as he caught Allie wrinkling her nose in response to the smell of the eggs. "Eccentric how?"

"He believes he was abducted by space aliens."

Allie kept peeling and dumped the last of the yolks into a bowl. "You have such interesting guests, Mom."

"I'll—" The ring of the doorbell silenced her. "Oh, dear, someone came early." She was in her usual anxious state before a meal was to be served. Though a perfect hostess, she always fretted until the first fork dipped into her food. "And I'm not ready, and there's so much left to do," she said, rushing from the room.

"She's still wonderful," Riley said when Janet disappeared.

Allie knew they'd formed a mutual admiration society. When living with him, she'd been thrilled that her mother and he had gotten along so well. Now their closeness made her feel ganged up on. Looking over her shoulder, she saw him viewing the food displayed on the counter. Often he'd commented about feeling stuffed after dinner at her mother's. "Going to show some restraint this time?"

"That's not easy," he said with a laugh. "Your mother still puts out one hell of a meal."

Allie opened the refrigerator and retrieved a bag of tomatoes and a bottle of beer. "Why don't you tell me what you and my mother were talking about?" she said, handing the bottle, now uncapped, to him.

Riley took a swig of the beer. He didn't bother to deny what had been so obvious. "You. She said you're like your father."

Rummaging in a cabinet for the cutting board, Allie frowned at him over her shoulder. "How am I like him?"

"When he got an idea in his head, he'd never let it go. She thinks that's the problem with us. You think it's all or nothing between us."

"And what, exactly, do you think?" she asked, definitely curious about what he'd say.

"We could compromise."

Allie couldn't comprehend any compromise. They had different goals in life. She washed the tomatoes, as amazed that her mother had mentioned her father as she was with this conversation.

Her mother had always avoided discussing Allie's father after their separation. Even before it, he'd rarely been home, rarely been a part of their lives. Vividly, Allie recalled the last night she'd seen her father. He'd been a tall man, good-looking, with reddish brown hair cut short, military style. In her pajamas, she'd crept down the steps because she'd heard her parents arguing. Nine years old, she'd clung to the banister, not wanting to be seen, and had watched him leave. He'd died while away. A ruptured appendix. "I'm surprised Mom said anything about him."

Riley accepted the cutting board and a knife. He knew the story. One night while in his arms, she'd revealed a child's heartbreak to him. She'd overheard an argument, had heard her father admit he didn't want the responsibility of a family. And she'd believed that if it hadn't been for her, her mother wouldn't have asked him for a divorce.

"She has memories, too, Allie. They come back when you don't expect them, don't they?"

She knew Riley was talking about them now. "They do," she agreed honestly.

"Some we want." He paused in slicing a tomato and set down the knife. "Some we don't want."

Allie's heart jerked as he stepped close behind her. *Don't touch me. Please don't touch me,* she silently begged. Of course, he didn't hear her plea. Featherlight, his fingers brushed aside the hair at the nape of her neck. No protest escaped her lips, even though she felt the heat of his breath close to her ear.

He heard her strangled sigh, felt her soften against him. "I keep wondering about that phone call you made to me. What might have happened." Lightly he trailed a finger down the side of her throat. "I'm sorry I hurt you." He wanted to kiss her. He wanted one more kiss, then maybe, just maybe, he could walk away.

"Allie, we need the rest of the steaks, and—oh!" In a movement so awkward it seemed comical, her mother tossed up her hands as if a robber had insisted on it. "I have such awful timing, don't I? I'm sorry," she said, as if certain she'd intruded.

"Mother, if you take one step away..." Allie threatened, but had no idea what might follow those words.

Pivoting, Riley snatched his beer from the counter. "Nothing wrong with your timing, darling," he said to ease her discomfort. "You saved me. I think she was looking for slave labor."

Janet gave him a semblance of a smile, a rueful one, and set a neighbor's shrimp salad on the counter. "A few guests are in the backyard already." She tipped her head toward the screen door, through which people sitting at the redwood picnic tables were visible. "Come out when you're ready." In passing, she touched Riley's arm in an apologetic gesture.

Allie could have thanked her mother. She'd been close, too close, to forgetting what she had to remember when around him. "She's really happy to see you," she assured him while nudging the bowl of shrimp salad onto an already crowded refrigerator shelf. "I'll finish stuffing these eggs, then we can join them." Though certain her mother was keeping an eye on Devin, Allie knew the moment had come for her to step outside and lift Devin in her arms, for Riley to see his son. "All done with the tomatoes?"

"Yeah."

His answer was overshadowed by banging on the screen door.

"Ma-ma." Standing on the porch, Devin banged with his usual tenacity.

Stunned. Allie could think of no other word to describe Riley's expression.

"Mama?" His eyes, filled with questions, darted from her to Devin, who'd grown more persistent.

All the yesterdays seemed to flutter away for Allie. She opened the door for Devin and ushered him in. "This is Devin," she said, gathering him in her arms. Shy around strangers, he turned his face into her neck for a second—only a second. His own curiosity about a stranger made him look up.

Riley studied him. He possessed Allie's dimples, reddish blond hair and brown eyes. He looked like Allie. More had changed than Riley had been prepared for. She had a son. Was this what she'd meant when she'd said she was different? "You did a hell of a lot more than get married. You're a mother?"

She couldn't help it; she laughed. She had expected to feel edgy when this moment came. Instead she felt remarkably relaxed, as if some weight had been lifted from her. She set Devin down. "Yes, I'm a mother."

"Dink." Devin insisted, stretching on toes toward the sink.

Allie filled a plastic glass with water and handed it to him.

"Ice ceam. Ice ceam," Devin chanted.

With a little cajoling, Allie soothed his demand for his favorite food. She understood her son. His father remained the mystery to her. She'd always wondered if Riley had numbed a place within himself to make it unreachable. "I have to run these outside," she said about the casserole of baked beans and a relish tray. Hands full, she paused in the doorway, holding the screen door open with her back. Time for retreat, she decided, and urged Devin to come out the door with her.

Looking back, she saw Riley still leaning against the counter—head bent, deep in thought and frowning. She lingered for another moment. Deep down she wished, she prayed, for the impossible—that he would have seen himself in his son.

Chapter Five

Riley didn't move. He'd thought he'd known everything about her, every nuance. But the woman he'd touched and loved, the one whose body was as familiar as his own—the woman who tidied the apartment in the morning before leaving for work in case there was a fire, who'd told him at the beginning of their relationship that she wanted nothing that would make either of them feel trapped—had become a mother.

Until that sudden announcement about marriage and kids on the last night they'd been together, she'd never indicated that she wanted all that he'd shunned. Had she lied because she knew that's what he wanted? Had she been convincing herself of something that went against her own dreams and wishes?

And then what? One day had she suddenly awakened, knowing she couldn't live that life anymore?

Tension was pulling at the back of his neck, and he raised a hand to rub the area. She'd been right: she wasn't the same anymore. She suddenly belonged on his Don't Touch list.

He couldn't pinpoint feelings about her having a child. The boy was older than a year—fourteen, fifteen months. Riley didn't know how to judge a kid's age. But logic told him she'd met Mitch Anderson, married and gotten pregnant almost immediately after their own breakup.

If he had an ounce of good sense, he'd leave. A mother. He shook his head in disbelief, still grappling to accept that particular change in Allie's life as he stepped outside.

Feeling lost in a fog, he followed the zany, white-haired professor to the buffet table. The man bent his ear about his close-encounter experience. Though Riley could have sat anywhere, he searched out Allie and chose a seat at the table beside her. Instead of her, he stared at her son in his high chair. *Her son.* The words seemed to be in a foreign language.

"You're quiet," Allie said, not bothering to pick up her fork.

With a humorless laugh, he shook his head. "I can't say I ever expected this."

"This?"

"You having a child." He felt betrayed. That he did seemed ridiculous. He'd never wanted a kid, so why should he feel this way because she'd had one?

He'd known there had been a husband. Marriage, then kids—they went hand in hand. It was a package that he'd resisted.

Allie didn't bother to look at him. She wanted to scream at him, *This is your son.* Her heart constricted that he wasn't even questioning the possibility that Devin might be his. Briefly she paused in eating to help Devin stab his little fork into a potato chunk. How could Riley not see himself in Devin's smile? Because he didn't want to.

As Devin took back his fork and stabbed at the food with the fierce independence she'd encountered often, Allie started eating. Riley had to understand now what she'd been trying to tell him.

They lived in different worlds. Hers revolved around diapers and baby teeth and early bedtimes, because Devin bounded around the house at the first light of dawn. Riley's meant eating dinner from a jar of peanut butter, spending the night on his boat, sleeping in late.

Her life meant thinking of what was best for her son. A child made people give their thoughts, their heart, their love to another. Riley rarely shared himself.

She'd always known that, always believed that Devin didn't need a father charging into his life out of a sense of duty, that he deserved more.

Hearing her mother's laughter, Allie pulled herself from her thoughts. For the sake of her mother's party, she would somehow manage to keep a smile in place. "Have you talked to the professor yet?" she asked, to halt more uneasiness between her and Riley.

"I've talked to him."

Allie traced his stare to Devin. Having grown impatient with his fork, he was stuffing potato salad into his mouth with his fingers.

"He gave me an accounting of his flight in a UFO." Why hadn't she told him before that she had a son? Riley turned his frown on Janet, who was approaching.

"Allie, there's someone to see you." A worried look accompanied her mother's words. "Jason," she whispered, almost hissing his name. "I left him in the living room."

Riley heard part of the conversation—the "him in the living room" part. Allie had claimed Neubocker and she were friends, but... He couldn't stop himself. Logic told him that he had no rights, but the feeling sweeping over him was far more emotional. It was good old-fashioned jealousy.

While Allie lifted Devin from his high chair, Riley decided a private conversation with Neubocker might provide insight about his relationship with Allie.

At the arched entrance to the dining room, he stopped. Instead of Neubocker, another guy waited in the living room on Janet's tweed sofa. Riley didn't like him on sight. He supposed that if he had to categorize him, he'd rank him as great looking—a tall, dark-haired guy with a cleft in his chin. Some women had a thing for those.

Hearing the screen door slam, the guy raised his head. Briefly, his gaze clashed with Riley's.

No, he definitely didn't like him, Riley mused.

And by the look he'd received, he guessed the feeling was mutual.

Before Allie appeared, Riley slipped into Janet's study. Though he'd never intended to eavesdrop, he was tempted.

The day was steadily growing worse, Allie decided as Jason stormed out of the house within minutes of their confrontation. He'd had his say, had issued his demands and had left her with more trouble to handle.

Stopping in the kitchen, she heard Devin's gleeful squeal at hitting a baseball and wandered to the door to watch him.

He dropped his red bat, and with short little steps, darted across the lawn. From the time he was ten months old, he'd chosen a baseball bat as his favorite toy. In a hit-and-miss manner, he swung at the ball on a colorful red-and-yellow batting tee, the perfect height for toddlers. As the ball flew a few feet, he dropped his bat and took off running again in a haphazard circle before returning to the tee and clapping his hands gleefully.

She smiled and turned away from the door. He loved baseball. Like his father. During a quiet moment alone, Riley had revealed to her that he'd envisioned a professional baseball career. He'd also told her that he'd forgotten that ambition when he'd turned sixteen, when his parents had died. She'd always wondered how many other dreams he'd abandoned that year. He would never tell her, would never talk about his family or his childhood. To anyone who asked about his past, he recounted experiences on the police force, as if that had been the beginning of his life.

In a way, she understood. Sometimes one event turned a person's life around. Devin's birth had been like a beginning for her, too.

Since several desserts were already gone from the kitchen counter, Allie opened the refrigerator and reached for the cheesecake, then stepped outside. Her stride faltered feet from the table she'd been seated at. Though some guests were standing, most were still seated. All it took was one quick scan to know Riley wasn't among them.

So he'd left. Disappointment knotted her throat.

"I'm supposed to get a pie server from you."

She blinked hard before focusing on Professor Rowdy, stationed in front of the dessert table. Allie gave him a slim smile and set down the cheesecake. "Were you volunteered for that job?"

"Actually, yes. Your mother asked your beau to get it."

Allie felt a tide of amusement wash through her at his choice of word.

"But he volunteered me because he had something else to do," the man finished. With his white frizzy hair, he certainly had the absentminded-professor look. "I agreed he was more capable of retrieving a ball from the roof than I was."

When he gestured behind her, Allie swung around. Nothing prepared her for the sight of Riley on the roof, holding Devin's ball.

"He said he'd better get it, since he helped him hit it up there."

He hadn't left. Joy threatened to swarm in on her as she saw her son's beaming face when Riley jumped down and handed the ball to him. She'd thought he would flee at the first opportunity. Instead he'd stayed. He'd done better than that.. He'd been spending time with Devin.

Briefly her eyes met Riley's. He had no idea of the impact he was having on her by playing with Devin. "Thank you," she said, approaching him.

He saw a look in her eyes he didn't like, as if he'd done something wonderful. "It was no big deal."

It was to her, but she kept the thought to herself.

"He got quite a hit." He laughed, remembering how it had felt to have his hands on the boy's small ones, remembering the joy in those dark eyes when the ball had taken flight.

"*He* got quite a hit?" she teased, taking a seat at one of the picnic benches to watch Devin, now delighted with a small blue bottle of bubbles he'd found.

The moment felt unnatural to Riley. He didn't talk about kids, had never really paid attention to them.

Beside Allie, Devin blew, spitting at air. His brows knitting, he looked up at her in puzzlement. "Let's try this." She dipped the wand that Devin was holding into the bottle and waved his arm.

His face lit with delight as several golf-ball-size bubbles floated in the air. "Bub-bles."

"Was your unexpected visitor the brother-in-law?" Riley asked, deciding that subject was safer.

Allie shot a look of disbelief at him. "How did you...?" She didn't bother to veil the astonishment sweeping through her. "You followed me?"

"No, I checked him out before you came in."

Allie decided that Riley didn't look the least bit apologetic.

"I wondered if it was Neubocker again."

Perhaps because he'd done so much already that had pleased her, Allie couldn't scrape up any annoyance with him.

"He's kind of stuffy, isn't he?" He didn't wait for an answer and offered his opinion. "Not exactly the kind to bring into a kid's life."

Her heart thudded. She'd seen a flare of discomfort in his eyes when they'd been talking about Devin, had expected him to pretend Devin was nonexistent now. "I don't plan to. Anyway, he's taken."

"Taken?"

Enough, Allie decided. "There's another woman. In fact, he's almost engaged—"

"He's cheating?" Neubocker had looked like the true-blue, faithful type to him.

"No, of course not." Why were they even discussing Stefan? "He's been with Rebecca for six years."

Riley pondered that for a second. Neubocker was a slow-moving man. "Doesn't it bother her that he's taken you out?"

"You are so suspicious. Rebecca is out of town, studying the effects of ozone depletion on the rain forests. He has a very open and honest relationship with her." Something Allie and Riley had never had because of him. "She knows he's taken me to auctions. Only auctions," Allie clarified. "They've become very good friends of mine."

Riley set a booted foot on the bench she was sitting on. "The brother-in-law is a different story, isn't he?"

It amazed her that Riley wanted to know everything when he gave nothing of himself. "He's my problem," Allie said firmly.

Her message was clear: back off.

She watched his gaze narrow on hers as if he was trying to see inside her. She could have told him more, but the cop in him would feel some need to help. He'd hate knowing what seemed so obvious about himself. He was a rescuer, someone who involved himself in others' problems to save them. Why he never recognized that about himself puzzled her. But she doubted he'd like having it pointed out to him. And she wasn't interested in Riley Garrison, the cop, being in her life. She wanted the man.

Silently she groaned at the admission that had unwittingly slipped through. "I can handle this," she said, purposely sounding less defensive in order to end the conversation about Jason.

Standing, she surveyed the tables. "Don't break any windows playing ball while I'm gone," she teased before stepping away to carry dishes into the kitchen.

Riley watched her stroll away. It was time to leave. A wiser man would have gone sooner. He'd only come to satisfy a curiosity, to see if he could feel the same warm welcoming sensation he'd known before when he'd been with Allie at Janet's. It seemed stronger than ever, he admitted as he made his way to the screen door.

At the sink rinsing dishes, Allie heard the door slam and looked over her shoulder.

"I'm going. Janet was in the middle of a conversation." He took a step closer. "Thank her for me."

"I will." How polite to each other they sounded. How close he suddenly was. Too close. She made a move to step away, on the pretense of reaching for a dish towel. She never took the step. He caught her arm, bringing their faces close, her body against his.

He felt her tense, but she didn't push him away. "What are you afraid of? Me?"

Was she breathing? she wondered. With his mouth so close that his breath warmed her face, she was spellbound. "Myself. That's what I'm afraid of." She nearly closed her eyes when his fingertips traced the side of her throat, the line of her jaw. "I keep forgetting what you aren't facing."

He didn't want to talk. He'd forgotten how much he'd dreamed of touching her skin, of feeling her slim body straining against him. He wanted to fill himself with her taste, her sweetness. "And what's that?"

"You don't want what I have in my life. And I need what you don't want—stability." She spoke the words, a tiny thread of anticipation holding her still. With all her heart, she wanted him to tell her that wasn't true. "I need it for Devin," she added. "He's important."

With his hand at the small of her back, Riley drew

her closer until he felt the length of her against him. "You think I don't know you're right?" It amazed him that she still felt so perfect against him. "But none of that seems to matter," he murmured, his annoyance not with her but with the truth in her words. "Nothing matters. Nothing matters but you."

Allie struggled for breath and braced herself, certain she was ready for this moment. She rarely lied to herself and wouldn't now. She wanted to be in his embrace, to savor the warmth of his mouth just one more time.

As his fingers tunneled into her hair, his mouth captured hers. A soft sigh escaped from her throat. Her mouth responded as it always had to the firm pressure of his lips, the moist warmth of his tongue.

The kiss was slow, deep, spreading an ache through her, reminding her of all she'd felt with him, all she'd ever wanted.

Eyes closing, she revisited a time two years ago, a time when she'd been younger, in love and uninhibited by responsibilities. Those were months when only he had mattered, when only the joy she'd felt every day she was with him had counted.

But memories paled in comparison to the moment. Wanting and desire slithered through her. One kiss sparked emotions of when his mouth had offered so much pleasure, when his tongue had taunted her breasts, raced down her skin, aroused a heat until shivers of need had raced through her. Like then, she wanted to weep with the intensity of her desire for him.

It was more than a kiss, she realized. Almost desperately, their mouths clung, as if they were trying to make up for lost years. She released a soft moan, feeling as if she'd been starved for him. Everything was so familiar, so right.

Her pulse pounding, she floated in the dream, which seemed within her grasp. She strained against him, eager, wanting, yearning again for the slick texture of his damp skin beneath her fingers. But so much was still wrong, her mind screamed. Too wrong.

A breath away from opening her heart to him, she tore her mouth from his. She had to remember the tears shed, the dreams lost, the pain endured. ''I can't do this,'' she barely managed to gasp. ''I have to think about tomorrows.''

''To hell with tomorrows,'' he said, in a voice so steady he amazed himself. ''If you tell me that you don't have any regrets about us, I'll leave you alone.'' During those few moments, when her mouth had been on his, he'd felt layer by layer of resistance dissolving. He believed, that, like him, she regretted a great deal.

Her breath unsteady, she nearly swayed when he released her and stepped away. Pressing her back to the closest wall, she steeled herself against the craving to fall into his arms again—to take, to give.

Impatience urged him to pull her near once more. He made himself move to the screen door. ''No answer?'' He wanted her to yell at him to get out of her life, but he knew that wouldn't do any good. He was back in it, and he wasn't about to get out of it yet. ''I want time with you again.''

Anxiety curled inside her. She'd been so sure he would back away when he saw Devin.

"I want you. You want me." The heat of her mouth lingered on his. "Let's start there."

She shouldn't agree, but she couldn't get the words out to argue.

As if needing contact with something, he placed a hand on the screen door, but still didn't push it open. "Have you taken Devin to the zoo here yet?"

"The zoo?" The question threw her off balance. Zoos were for families. "No, I haven't."

"Tomorrow then. Let's take him. I'll pick you up at ten."

He didn't wait for an answer. She doubted she could have uttered a sensible word. With a soft moan, she slouched against the counter, totally confused. What was happening? Why would he suggest an outing that included Devin?

Because Devin slept late the next morning, it allowed Allie the luxury of a long, relaxing bath. A dozen tasks needed her attention, including a basket of laundry.

With her hair pinned up, she sank to her neck in the steamy bath water and closed her eyes. Nervousness about the day ahead shadowed her while she dressed. Viewing her reflection in the snug white shorts, she stripped them off. No sense in adding fuel to the fire. She chose a yellow T-shirt and jeans, then pulled back her hair.

Today the three of them would be together, like a family. Was this the fantasy of a single mother, who stood alone so much, watching over her child? Often Allie had yearned for someone special who'd shoulder some of her problems, for someone who'd welcome the joys of parenting and feel, too, swelling pride whenever Devin did something exciting and new.

But she hadn't bothered to search for a man who'd understand that she came with her son as a package deal. After Mitch, she'd resigned herself to raising Devin alone. It occurred to her that she wasn't alone, except by choice. A man existed who'd fit perfectly into her life—and Devin's, if he wanted to.

She glanced at the clock, not for the first time, expecting Riley's phone call and some excuse so he could back away from a day with her and her son.

At three minutes to ten, she heard instead the ring of the doorbell. Edgy, she whipped around and nearly banged into her mother's entertainment center. Muttering to herself, she went to the door. She'd been off-kilter ever since she'd stepped from that leisurely bath. She'd knocked over Devin's orange juice, nearly dropped his folded high chair on her foot and was so disturbed that she'd even put Devin's diaper on backward.

What was even crazier, she felt breathless when she opened the door. This wasn't how she was supposed to feel. "I'm running late." She swung away, leaving Riley at the open door. "It's my own fault. I'll have Devin ready in a minute." She rambled on, not unaware of her own nervousness. With a look over her shoulder, she swept her arm toward Devin's car seat and stroller. "You might want to put those in your car. But I have to make a phone call before we can leave.''

He smiled at the trace of self-disgust that he heard in her voice, at the small show of nerves, at the way she looked. Younger. Cute with her hair damp at the ends and a faint spray of freckles on her nose visible without makeup. "You're not on a schedule," he said to the air as she breezed out of the room. But she was. A built-in one. To dawdle went against her basic nature.

For old times' sake, he wandered to the living room to settle in the comfortable beige chair her mother owned. He'd staked a claim to it often enough after one of Janet's dinners had left him feeling stuffed. Memories. They existed everywhere. Taking one step into the living room, he laughed. A little boy already occupied the chair.

Devin gave him that infectious grin of his, then in an awkward scrambling movement, slid off the chair to barrel toward Riley. "Up."

What Riley interpreted as an expectant look settled on the round face. Glancing around, he searched for a rescuer. No Allie, no Janet. Helping Devin hit a few baseballs had been easy, but he had no idea what to do with a kid this age.

"Up! Up!" Devin insisted, holding arms out to him.

You're bigger than him, Riley reminded himself. Vaguely he recalled his younger sister, then his brother around this age, but his parents had been alive then, and his whole world had centered on making a home run at his Little League game.

Plopping on the chair, he lifted Devin onto his lap. Allie's son. The small body against his felt breakable. Riley remembered how slight another boy's body had felt. The last time he'd seen his brother, he'd been thin and wiry. Like him, Devin clamped a small hand at the back of Riley's neck. No artificial scent clung to his hair. He smelled clean, fresher than anything Riley could think of.

"Can you say Riley?" *Brilliant, Garrison.*

The toddler's fair brows dipped in the semblance of a frown. "Ily?"

Riley laughed. "Yeah, Ily." Devin's eyes stayed on him. Smiling eyes, eyes so much like Allie's that it hurt to look at them. Something in the vicinity of his heart fluttered. Dumb, he mused. He wasn't sentimental by nature. So why was the sound of the unique, abbreviated name having such an effect on him?

"Book." Grinning, Devin held a picture book close to Riley's face. "Book."

Riley returned what he was sure was an idiotic grin. A few years back, he'd delivered a baby in the back seat of a car. It had been an experience that had left him drained, sweating and awed. But he'd held the baby only for a second.

"Book," Devin announced again, with more persistence, and held it out to him. Then one little finger pointed at a picture. "Bot."

Riley grinned. "Boat," he repeated. This might not be too hard, with that little finger as a guide.

In the kitchen, Allie scribbled the phone number for a handyman on a sheet of paper. It was silly to be so nervous. This wasn't a first date. She knew Riley better than any man, even Mitch. She knew he had moods, some dark, silent ones. She knew how quickly he was prone to laughter, especially at himself. She'd cooked meals, critiqued movies, walked in the snow with him. He was no stranger, but all of that had happened before Devin. Today would be a first.

She pulled her hair away from her face, securing it with a ribbon. When she'd left Devin, he'd been entranced in front of the television, watching his favorite dinosaur dancing and singing. Because she'd checked on him on her way to the kitchen, she expected to see him dancing or imitating robot moves or clapping to some song.

Again she was thrown off balance.

All the steadiness she'd gathered since leaving Riley slithered away. Her heart lurched at the sight of her son cuddled in Riley's arms.

"Is something...?" Behind Allie, her mother halted abruptly. "Why did you stop?" Her voice dropped to a whisper. "Oh, Allie."

Don't say anything, Allie nearly begged, not now. She needed a few seconds. Emotion hummed through her at seeing them together like that. It thrilled her; it pained her. Unsteady, her stomach knotting, she crossed the distance to them.

Devin giggled over the sound of Riley's quacking.

"Duck," Devin said.

"Right." Riley pointed to the picture. "That's a duck. You're pretty smart."

At the softness in his voice, Devin responded with another prize-winning grin.

Doubts fluttered through Allie. What if she'd made the biggest mistake of her life in keeping them apart? She stepped forward, despising the uncertainty within her.

"Ready to go?" he asked, looking up at her.

"Almost." She averted her gaze, wanting to look anywhere but at them—together. "I have to make a phone call." She reached for the telephone book. Her eyes burned from concentration as she stared at the print on one page. Just because he'd spent a few one-on-one moments with his son didn't mean he'd welcome fatherhood.

"Emergency?"

"Sort of. There's a hole in one wall at the shop." Act normal. "One strategically hidden by the player piano."

"How did it happen?"

Allie reached for the receiver. "Mitch put his fist through it."

Riley slanted a hard look at her. "Did he just punch walls?"

She guessed his thoughts. "Yes. Just walls."

"So why did he punch it?"

"Frustration. Exasperation. I'm not sure which. His brother, Jason, had just left. I'd heard my name tossed around during their argument. We'd visited him to tell him we were getting married." She glanced at the opened phone book again. "He wasn't happy."

"First meeting?"

Allie looked up and nodded.

"He didn't know you," he said, running his large hand over the top of Devin's head.

The touch seemed so gentle, so loving. She gave him a slim smile. "Jason isn't the most open-minded person in the world."

"Jerk."

Struggling to keep deeper emotions at bay, she grasped at amusement like a lifeline. "Still make snap judgments?" she teased.

Shrugging, he released his hold on a wiggling Devin to let him scramble off his lap. The day might not be as difficult as he'd anticipated. He liked the boy. Better than that, Devin seemed to like him. "I don't need to know him better." Standing, Riley closed the distance to Allie and cupped a hand around the back of her neck. "I know you."

He delivered a quick kiss, then turned his back to her and lifted the stroller and the car seat. Allie closed her eyes. *You don't know me.* He would never see her as deceptive, but omission of truth was as good as a lie, wasn't it?

Chapter Six

With school out, hoards of children packed the zoo, young couples ambled past exhibits pushing strollers, preschoolers in day-care groups held hands.

The warmth of the sun blasted against flesh. Pausing while people climbed into one of the safari trains that circled the zoo, Allie pointed in the direction of the gorillas. "I think the elephants are that way, too."

Riley had never been to a zoo. At least, he never remembered going. It was a place for kids, families. Not his kind of place, yet here he was. Hell, he'd suggested this cozy family outing instead of a romantic evening alone with her at a quiet, intimate restaurant. He couldn't say why, except the boy was part of her life. Too important to her to be excluded. "Did you get a repair man for that hole in the wall?"

"No. The one my mother suggested didn't answer the phone."

Another time, she wouldn't have hesitated to share her worry with Riley. He was a good listener. Hadn't he listened quietly to her concern before her mother's hysterectomy, her anxiousness when she'd contemplated returning to college?

A group of Girl Scouts made her pause on the path. "It's crowded," she said with a laugh, nudging the stroller forward. When Devin pointed at the elephant, she stopped so he could watch.

The earthy smells of the animals permeated the air. As one of the elephants dipped its trunk in a pond and squirted water in the air, Devin giggled and swiveled to look up at her. "Ber?"

Allie laughed and bent down to his level. No matter what was wrong in her life, how tired she was or what was worrying her, he made her laugh. "No, not a bear. An elephant," she said, enunciating slowly, aware his eyes were watching her mouth. "Lately he works so hard to copy what I say."

Riley leaned on the rail beside her. "He's sweet, Allie." A need to touch her son overwhelmed him. He wasn't sure why. He'd been around the kids of other detectives and had never felt any connection. Was he feeling this way because Devin was her child? Lightly he stroked the top of Devin's head. "Was your husband blond?"

Allie had seen his caress. Could he feel in some mysterious way a closeness with Devin?

"Allie?"

She tensed, aware that he was waiting for an answer. Her mind gathered thoughts, sorted through them, tossed some aside. He'd met Jason, knew he was dark haired. Mitch had been, too. "No," she answered. "A lot of children start out as blondes and their hair darkens later."

"Was it a good marriage?" Elbows on the railing, he kept staring at the elephant.

Allie sighed, then admitted. "It wasn't perfect."

Riley damned himself for wanting to hear her say those words. "There was trouble?"

Restless, she moved her shoulders. "From the beginning, it was never right. We fought over little things."

That bothered her a lot, Riley guessed. He knew about the final argument between her parents. It had had a lasting effect on her. She hated confrontation of any kind.

"Too many nights he'd come home late. He'd been drinking," Allie continued, pushing the stroller toward the next exhibit. "It got worse. He gambled." She tried to speak without emotion while she recalled the terrible days and nights. "I never knew that about him," she admitted, "but he was compulsive, one of those people who couldn't resist betting on anything and everything." A breeze tore at her hair. "I told him I'd go back to Chicago with him. I thought if he got away from people he'd met in Seattle, got interested in his store again, everything would be better."

Allie watched two pigeons picking for food on the walking trail. "He didn't want to leave Seattle." She hadn't understood Mitch then. Later, she'd zeroed in on the reason for his reluctance. A weak man, he'd always been under his brother's thumb. "Because my mother was here, I wanted to move back. When we returned to Chicago, he was constantly drinking, constantly gambling. We talked about divorce before he died," she admitted.

Around them, the squawking of birds, the squeals of kids filled the air. Allie watched a vulture in an aviary soar from one leafless limb to another and thought of Jason. "I finally understood what was wrong. By coming back, he had to answer to Jason again."

During the months after Mitch died, she'd relieved herself of guilt and accepted that she'd married an immature man who'd found what he'd believed was freedom from an overbearing brother. Perhaps she had been his excuse to stay in Seattle, to be away from Jason. Perhaps he'd used her, too. In the end, though, he'd self-destructed.

Riley trailed her, not knowing what to say. He'd been miserable after she'd left, had wanted that for her, too. But not so much pain. She'd spoken easily about a time that he guessed had been hell for her.

On the winding path, Allie paused at an area of swampy marsh that led to an enclosed pond of murky green water. Alligators were so still they appeared unreal.

"Algatr," Devin said, but looked away as if bored with them. Monkeys appealed to him more. So did the giraffes, and the hot dog she got him for lunch later.

Seated at one of the picnic tables, Allie stretched

across the space between them to reach for the ketchup packets. Funny how the most minuscule thing could snap forward a memory. "When did you stop pouring ketchup over everything?" she asked, angling a look at Riley.

"I never ruined your mother's cooking or yours with ketchup," he reminded her.

"You did the first time I cooked for you."

"I didn't want to hurt your feelings and not eat it if it was bad."

Squeezing ketchup from the packet onto her hot dog, Allie slanted a smile at him. "So you were bound and determined to be polite at all costs?"

He saw the vague smile curving the corners of her mouth. "Politeness had nothing to do with it. I wanted you in bed," he murmured in a low voice.

"Incorrigible," she said with a soft laugh.

"Yeah, I know." As a gentle breeze whipped around them and blew her hair forward around her face, he reached out to tuck strands behind her ear, wanting some contact with her. His eyes never left hers. He'd begun to understand the fragile tightrope he was walking with her. "I'm glad I was."

Allie looked down at the hot dog before her. Effortlessly he could sweep all sensibility away from her, make her yearn for what could never be. "You endured five more meals before that happened."

"But you're a wonderful cook. So it was…" He paused and chuckled with a remembrance. "It was pure torture." He wanted to kiss her right now, right here in front of strangers, in front of a little boy who existed because of her. His body felt tense, his stomach tight as he drew in the scent of her fragrance, one that had haunted him, intruding when he'd been with any other woman. Allie was in his blood, would always be. Across the table, he laced his fingers with her. *I missed you.* He wanted to tell her, but couldn't get the words out.

In silence, they finished eating. Wiping her hands on a napkin first, Allie bent over to dab at the ketchup on Devin's cheek.

"Duck!" Devin squealed excitedly at one emerging from the nearby pond. His little arms raised with his eagerness to get out of the stroller and chase a duck that had waddled onto the grass.

Riley smiled and pivoted away to slip coins in a box filled with food for the birds. There was such innocence at that age. But he'd seen sadness, anguish in the eyes of kids not much older than Devin. "Here." He faced Allie and dumped the seed in her open palm.

"Thank you." She tossed the food toward a mallard duck.

"There's a concert in the park. Do you want to take Devin there? Will he sit long enough?" Riley asked, feeling like a bumbling fool with all the questions.

Allie paused in throwing the food. "He loves music. Any kind." She tossed the rest of the food. "Rap, country, classical." Other ducks swam, trailing the first one. It took courage to lead, Allie thought.

Bending down to look at Devin, she wiped a frown from her face. Did she have a right to keep Devin from Riley? Was it fair to her baby to bring his dad into his life? "We'd better go," she said, watching Devin yawn and rub an eye with his knuckles. *I'm sorry, Devin. I wish your mommy was smarter.* "He's getting sleepy."

If he was just needing a woman, he'd have no problem, Riley decided at seven the next morning. He was sure several women would be happy to get his phone call. They wouldn't block his advances at every turn. They wouldn't deny wanting him.

But they wouldn't do. No one would, except her.

With a disgusted sigh, he propped his feet on his desk and draped a telephone book across his lap. Grabbing at straws, he wondered again about the brother-in-law. In between thumbing pages, he eyed a rookie cop kicking a precinct vending machine, a notorious quarter thief.

Across the aisle from him, another detective swiveled in his chair. It squeaked loudly, but mingled with the discord of sounds in the precinct. "When's Vincetti coming back?"

Chin to his chest, Riley angled a look at Ted Porter. "He took two weeks."

Porter, a stout man ready for retirement and the relaxing life of fishing, frowned. "Why did he need that long off?"

"You're getting old. He's on his honeymoon." Riley dropped his booted feet from his desk, yanked open the bottom drawer of his desk and fumbled for a butterscotch in his stash of hard candy. "How long you been married?"

"Forty-one years."

Riley released a low whistle and snatched up a pencil to scribble an address. "You and your wife are an anachronism today."

"Hey!" Porter returned, as if he'd been called a foul name.

"How did you do that? Stay married that long?"

The corners of Porter's eyes crinkled with a network of lines. "We love each other."

"That simple?"

"Well, a little nuzzling helps."

Rising, Riley laughed. "Maybe you aren't too old, Porter."

He thought a little nuzzling would help him, too.

Twice he double-checked the address on the slip of paper in his pocket. Jason Anderson's store was in a high-class part of town off Michigan Avenue, wedged between an art gallery and a furrier.

Riley approached the antique shop's beveled-glass door. Against the backdrop of a black, oriental silk screen and tiered in the one large window were several enormous and intricately painted vases. What he knew about antiques and furnishings would fit into a thimble, but he'd gone to an auction with Allie after they'd first met. She'd pointed out a vase similar in appearance and had informed him that it was a rare collector piece from the Ming Dynasty.

Wary of making too quick of a movement, he paused just inside the shop. An ambience of simplicity and elegance surrounded him. Not seeing anyone, he turned to his left. As his leg brushed against a pedestal table, a huge statue on it wobbled. In a swift move, he snagged it before it tipped over.

"That's a life-size stoneware bust of Prince Rupert," a haughty voice said behind him.

Whatever politeness Riley came in with slithered away. Jason Anderson irritated the hell out of him. "I'm a friend of Allison Harrigan's."

"Yes, I know," he said in a more disdainful tone. "I recall seeing you at her mother's home."

Not one to exchange pleasantries he didn't feel, Riley announced simply, "You and I need to talk."

"I'm not surprised by your visit," Anderson said snidely, adjusting the bust on the ornate stand, though it hadn't really moved. "I assumed when I saw you, when you came into the room before her, that she'd found another to come to her defense."

Frustration weaved through Riley. What in the devil did that mean? "I want to know what's going on."

Anderson clucked his tongue. "I can't believe she hasn't poured her heart out to you. That would be so like her," he said with an air of arrogance. "I'm sure that's her usual procedure—to find someone to live off of."

Though not easily riled, Riley felt temper slice through him at the implication that Allie used people—namely Anderson's brother. Riley jammed his hands into his pockets to keep them from clenching. Only someone who didn't know her would suggest that. She was independent to a fault. "Quit talking in riddles."

Though he looked amused, Anderson released a

mirthless laugh. "Obviously you don't know her very well."

"I know her well enough."

"Do you? I doubt that, or you'd have heard the same tale of woe she gave my brother until he couldn't resist her."

Riley heaved an exasperated breath. Patience usually came easily to him, but Anderson was stretching it to the limit. "What tale of woe?"

"Oh, I'm not going to spoil her fun. Let her sucker you in. You look like you deserve it."

That did it. "I don't know what the hell you're talking about," Riley said in a slow, measured and calm manner that took effort. "But you're close— real close—to having your nose rearranged." He took a step forward and felt some satisfaction that the man reared back. "Get this straight," he said as quietly as he could. "Whatever is going on, be warned. She's not alone."

At mid-afternoon, the waiting room at the children's hospital was cheerful and bright with the sun pouring in. Toys in bright colors, mostly red and blue and green, were scattered over the carpet and between rows of chairs, wherever the last toddler had abandoned them. The clock on a wall behind the receptionist's counter moved with excruciating slowness.

Allie resisted twisting the straps of her shoulder bag. She'd done fairly well on appearing calm until a few minutes ago, when her mother had left to go to the rest room.

Alone, Allie had too much silence around her despite the wails of one youngster or another growing impatient at being in strange surroundings.

It's not major surgery, she reminded herself as a calming thought. A ten-minute procedure to put the tubes in Devin's ears, the doctor had told her. A fairly common procedure. *This is my son,* she'd wanted to scream. No assurances would alleviate maternal anxiety.

Close to getting up and pacing, she looked for a distraction. Head bent, she dug into her shoulder bag for mail that she'd jammed in and hadn't opened yet.

"You look as if you could use this."

Allie recognized the voice. Slowly she looked up from the foam cup in Riley's hand to meet his stare. "Who told you I was here?"

"Your mother." Taking a seat on a vinyl-and-chrome chair beside her, he uncapped the coffee. "I called her house." He'd wanted to find out what Anderson had meant. Instead he'd learned that they were leaving for the hospital. "She told me it's some kind of thing for his ears?"

"Devin's been getting a lot of ear infections. This should help."

Any questions nagging at him about Anderson faded. "Did something happen?" he asked softly, noting the telltale redness rimming her eyes.

"No," she assured him, accepting the coffee he offered.

She sounded firm, strong, but he wasn't fooled. "I hate to say the obvious. Why were you crying?"

"It's dumb." She gave her head a shake. "I was so worried he'd cry when I had to leave him."

That apprehension and not heartbreak had caused her crying relaxed him. "What's dumb about that?"

"Devin didn't cry. I did." She gave him a self-deprecating, weak smile.

He'd always known she was ninety-nine percent heart. Riley slid his hand over hers. "How long has it been?"

"Fifteen minutes." She took strength from the strong hand around hers. "They really make this as nice of an experience as they can for little ones. There's another room full of toys." Cautiously she sipped the steaming coffee. "After we got here, they gave me a yellow hospital gown for Devin, then they let him play in a room full of toys with others waiting to have the same operation," she said, with a glance toward a far door.

Lightly Riley squeezed her hand to soothe her anxiousness. He wished he was better at comforting, but he'd done so little of it.

"A nurse told me that I should be able to see him in about twenty minutes." Allie looked down as Riley's pager beeped. "Someone wants you, Detective." She gave him a slim smile. "There's a phone in the hallway."

He didn't want to leave her alone. "I'll be only a minute."

"My mother will be..." She didn't bother finishing the sentence as the doctor came through the door.

As she sprang to her feet, Riley rose. Peripherally,

he saw her mother hurrying through the glass entrance doors toward her daughter.

"He's doing really well," the doctor assured both of them.

Relieved, Allie let the tension ooze out of her. Those were the words she had needed to hear most of all.

The doctor gave her an understanding smile. "You can go in to him."

Allie started forward, then looked back at Riley. "I know you have to leave. Thank you for coming."

"I'll see you tomorrow."

Hurrying to the door to see Devin, Allie paused for a second and watched him leave. Frowning, she rushed toward her son.

By the time Devin was dressed and they were going out the door, except for his fascination with the plastic hospital bracelet on his wrist, he gave no indication anything different had happened to him.

But her own outlook had turned topsy-turvy, Allie realized during quiet moments alone. Riley couldn't have done anything that would have impressed her more. If he'd known Devin was his son, she'd have assumed he'd felt obligated to be there.

But he hadn't known, and he'd come anyway.

At nine o'clock the next morning, Riley balanced a carton of pizza on his palm and opened the door to Allie's store—deliberately slowly, so the bell wouldn't ring.

The sound of music, an upbeat, old-time rock 'n' roll tune, drew him to the rear of the store. Her slender back to him, Allie seemed lost to her surroundings, dancing, swaying her hips. She looked like a different person from the one he'd seen yesterday in the hospital.

Unable to do differently, for a long moment he stood still, watching her snug backside in the tight, washed-out jeans. God, he loved the way she moved. "Need a partner?"

Startled, Allie jumped and swung around. "How long have you been standing there?"

"Long enough." Long enough to wish they were somewhere else, alone. "How's Devin?"

"He was a little tired yesterday, but otherwise he was fine." She let out a long breath as warmth spread through her. Here in the light of day, even with his hands not on her, he was inching his way into her heart. As he kept staring at her, she gestured with her head at the pizza carton on the closest surface, an unopened crate. "What's that?"

"Breakfast."

"Pizza?" Looking away, she cracked a smile and saw a curious Carol peeking in and grinning like a Cheshire cat.

"There's pizza," Riley suggested to her.

"For breakfast?" Carol's nose wrinkled with distaste. "No one eats pizza for breakfast," she said as a parting thought.

Except him, Allie recalled. She'd seen him devour lemon meringue pie, leftover, cold beef stew, and after one bad night on homicide, he'd downed three scotches before dawn.

"Sure they do. Statistics show that—"

"Don't try," Allie said lightly. "I know you make up those statistics. I told her you were weird."

His lips spread in a pleased grin. "Guess you've been talking a lot about me."

"Sharing your idiosyncrasies," she said, not giving him an inch of satisfaction. "I told her you had a cast-iron stomach." Allie was as deadpan as possible, though a smile colored her voice.

His eyes gleamed with humor as he toyed with a strand of her hair.

"I also told her that you drive me crazy." With some finesse, Allie skirted away from his touch. "There's a microwave in the corner to heat the pizza." She kept walking, not letting him see her smile. Weak. He was definitely weakening her, and after he'd come to be with her at the hospital, she was beyond wanting to resist.

To Riley, her suggestion required too much effort so early in the morning, especially this morning. After leaving her at the hospital, he'd had a late night at a hotel, questioning guests about a homicide in an elevator.

Munching on cold pizza, he slouched in a chair. Sunlight bathed the room. On the windowsill, several green plants soaked up the morning sun's warmth. A nurturer, Allie had always insisted that plants, even those destined for the garbage can, only needed TLC. Whether consciously or not, he'd stopped offering that years ago to anyone. Then she'd come along, giving it so freely, regardless of the risk.

"Did you get a cup of coffee?"

As she breezed back into the room, he roused himself from the chair and dropped the pizza cradled in his fingers to a plate. "Sit. I'll get it." His back to her, he poured coffee into a cup, an obvious favorite of hers. On it, a cartoon character, looking frazzled and balancing a baby on her hip, was reaching for her coffee cup. The artist had chosen childishly printed letters to write Mommy. "Did you sell something to the woman?"

"Not this time, but she'll come back." Allie pressed a fingertip into the soil of one plant. "I don't mind browsers."

Did she view him as a browser, too? Two years ago, he'd taken in the sights, enjoyed one woman's smile, the touch of her hands, the heat of her body, but had been unwilling to make a commitment. And she'd found another who would.

"Once here, they return," Allie said off-handedly. When he held the pizza carton toward her, she shook her head. "I couldn't face a pepperoni so early in the morning. Anyway, I have too much to do."

"Like what?" Stepping up behind her, he pressed his lips lightly to the side of her neck. Ever since he'd walked into her shop, he'd wanted this closeness with her.

She felt an inevitable sensation move through her from the play of his lips. "Like get inventory out of the stockroom."

"Feel." Turning her in his arms, he lifted her hand and placed her fingers on his bicep. "Plenty of muscles."

"I noticed."

His eyes gleamed with amusement. "Did you?"

He had no idea how much she'd noticed.

"So I'll move what you need moved."

"But—"

"Don't start a sentence that way," he mumbled against her neck.

She nearly closed her eyes as his mouth brushed hers once, then again, as if testing. "And I have to call a painter," she barely managed to add.

"I'll paint."

She sighed when he kissed at the sensitive flesh below her earlobe. "But there's that hole to fix. I need—"

"Whatever you need," he murmured, "I'll do it. You got a real handyman here. Helped my dad knock out a wall and build a sewing room for my mother."

Allie made her sure she didn't react, but that was a first. He'd never volunteered information about his family before. "We should get busy."

"I am busy," he whispered, pressing light kisses along her jaw.

Smiling, Allie squirmed out of his arms while she still could.

For most of the day, Riley shoved furniture around the store. Bracing a shoulder against a nineteenth-century kitchen cupboard, he nudged it away from a back wall, then muscled the player piano aside to view the hole, which was the size of a baseball. Devin's daddy had had quite a temper. In all fairness, Riley recalled his own temptation to punch Jason Anderson.

"Can you fix it?" Allie asked, contemplating the hole.

"Said I would."

"Yes, but that was before you saw it."

"I brought some plaster with me, but I'll need paint."

Allie paused in reaching for candlesticks she'd sold yesterday that needed to be wrapped for shipment. "Get whatever you need, and I'll pay you back."

She'd never see a bill, but he didn't bother to argue.

With an assessing eye, she scanned her inventory. Jason underestimated her. He'd applied pressure, believing she'd crumble. Never, she mused while calculating the value of several bureaus, dining room sets and other furniture. She stopped at the mahogany bureau with its flat-topped writing surface and marquetry decoration on three drawers. It didn't matter that she'd hate to part with it. For her to succeed, everything would have to go.

In passing, she eyed several Civil War firearms locked in a glass case. To the right buyer, they might bring a premium price. Facing an inevitable fact, she considered the bureau again, and waited only until Carol was done with the customer before calling, "Carol, was it Mrs. Manford who was interested in this bureau?"

"I think so." Her eyes darted with puzzlement from Riley back to Allie. "But I thought you were keeping that?"

"I've changed my mind." Regret stormed through

her when she thought about giving it up, but she'd sacrifice without reluctance. In fact, she was counting on its sale to lift her out of this quagmire of debt. She'd already decided to see a printer, make advertising flyers for a sale. Because of Jason, she had no choice. She'd have to liquidate her inventory.

Riley waited until Carol moved out of earshot. "You've got financial trouble, don't you?"

"Business is slow," she admitted. With her meager savings and a good sale, she might solve the latest problem Jason had dumped in her lap. "I have some heavy-duty bills to pay."

Not ones made by her. When Riley had been living with her, she'd owned one credit card that she'd rarely used. Resting his forearm on top of the player piano, Riley leaned to the side to put his face in front of her. "Level with me."

Weary of the dilemma she was in, she longed for someone to share her problem with. "Come to the back room," she said, aware of customers nearby. With him following, she stepped behind her desk and opened a drawer. "This is what's happening with him." She handed Riley the IOU Mitch had written to Jason.

Riley shrugged. "Your husband owed his brother money?"

"I do. Mitch's debts are mine." She took the paper from him and set it back in the drawer.

"And he's demanding payment?"

"Jason doesn't care about the loan, not really. He wants this store back. He insists it rightfully belongs in his family. So he's pressured me to repay it within thirty days. If I don't, he can take the store from me.''

Riley muttered a few choice words under his breath.

As he straddled a chair, she took a seat on an adjacent one. "When Mitch had gambling debts to pay, he went to Jason for help. I'm planning a sale of everything in here. If I'm lucky, I'll get enough money to pay him back that way.'' What she wouldn't do was hand the store and all the inventory over to Jason without a fight.

Anger churned within Riley. She'd be left with nothing except the building. He clamped down an urge to draw her close. She didn't need sympathy, wouldn't want it. "What else don't I know?'' he questioned shrewdly.

Tell him now. Tell him the truth. Would he whip away with disgust because she hadn't told him sooner that Devin was his son? "Isn't that enough?'' she said with deliberate lightness, and stepped away, aware that the shop door had opened several times while she'd been talking to him.

When she went to greet a customer, Riley got up from the chair and wandered back to the wall with the hole. Secrets. She'd always claimed he was the one with them, but it seemed she had one, too, now.

Hearing Allie's laughter, he leaned forward and saw the pompous-looking Neubocker.

Neubocker's voice rose, conveying excitement. "Allison, you should have come to the auction.''

Muttering under his breath, Riley squeezed behind

a carousel horse and positioned himself in front of the wall with its gaping hole.

"Tell me what happened," she said with almost childlike enthusiasm.

"Thomas Paine's *Common Sense* sold for a little over a hundred thousand. And Bernice Cosworth bought every Staffordshire dog in sight."

"Any Van Briggles pottery?"

Using more force than necessary, Riley whacked at the wall, making the hole bigger. Allie had a lot in common with the rigid-backed, nose-in-the-air Neubocker. Too much.

"There's another one this evening," Neubocker said.

Riley paused and peered over the top of the horse's black mane.

He saw Allie smile and touch Neubocker's arm. "Thank you for the invitation, but I can't go, Stefan."

Satisfied, Riley watched Neubocker glance his way. "I see."

"Good riddance," Riley mumbled to the wall. Just business acquaintances. That's what she'd told him. He blew out a long breath and silently stewed until she strolled back to him. "Neubocker wasn't here long?"

"He wanted to tell me about an auction."

"Is that the only reason he came?"

Allie arched a brow at him. "Only reason?"

"You said nothing was going on with him."

Amused, Allie decided to enjoy the conversation.

"I thought we had this discussion before. Do you think I'd sleep with him *and* go out with you?"

He sensed he was treading on rocky ground. "No. But what you feel and what he feels might not be the same."

Oh, how well she knew that situation. "That does happen."

"So why does he keep looking at me like I'm butting in?"

"Does he do that?" she asked, averting her face to veil a grin.

"Yes, he does that."

Humor danced in her eyes. She couldn't believe they were having this conversation. "He doesn't like you."

"I got that impression, but I thought it was because he had the hots for you."

Allie struggled hard to smother a laugh. Such an uncontrollable response about anything seemed farfetched for Stefan.

"So why does he keeping hanging around?"

If he kept pushing, she'd back him into a corner, Allie decided. "He wants to know your intentions." The words rang with such old-fashioned stuffiness, Allie couldn't help giggling.

Riley watched her walk away and squatted again in front of the hole in the wall. Stefan had a straighter backbone than Riley had given him credit for. Intentions? That usually meant commitment, marriage, permanency.

Chapter Seven

It took several layers of plaster to repair the wall. Satisfied with the job, Riley rolled up the dropcloth he'd retrieved along with plaster from his car earlier. "It's almost dinnertime," he said, pausing beside Allie.

Looking up from stacking shipment invoices, she sent him an amused smile. "Are you looking for an invitation to dinner?"

"I'll take you out." He could offer her nothing but today, but he wanted, needed a yes. He wasn't certain where they were going, if anywhere, but he couldn't let go, not yet.

Allie could have said yes. Her mother would watch Devin, but she thought he needed a reminder. "Devin looks for me to come home."

"I'll drive you home to see him." He noticed that

the frown didn't lift from her face. "Scratch that idea. We'll take him with us." That wasn't exactly what he'd planned when he'd made the suggestion. He'd envisioned candlelight and a good steak, not a family place that served hamburgers and provided high chairs. But he was good at adjusting his plans. And he liked the boy.

"Why?" Allie had to ask.

"Why not?"

A breezy response. Quit looking for some hidden message, she railed at herself. No paternal aura was sweeping over him. "I'll be ready to leave in ten minutes."

She was as good as her word.

In his car five minutes later, she settled back in the seat to enjoy the ride and relax. She couldn't; an excitement that had nothing to do with him snapped her forward in her seat. "Riley, stop!" she yelled as she spotted a handwritten sign mounted on a lamp-post.

"Stop?"

"Stop," she insisted.

He slammed on the brake. "What's the matter?"

Whipped forward in the seat belt, Allie uncurled her fingers from the dashboard and took a leveling breath. "Nothing is wrong," she assured him.

As she started to open the car door, he grabbed her arm. Had she changed her mind? "Where are you going?"

"That way."

In the second he took to look up, she slipped free of his grasp and got out of his car. Seeing her headed down an alley, he yanked the key from the ignition with a curse. By the time he rounded the front of the car, she was making a turn. "What are you doing?" he asked when he caught up with her.

"I want to see what's there." She pointed at the posted sign on a lamppost. "There's a moving sale."

"You have no idea what you're going to run into here."

"Treasures." Gleefully, like a kid rushing into a toy store, she veered toward a stranger's garage.

Riley gave up arguing and followed. He found her standing beside one of the rickety tables scattered about the garage. "What are you looking for?" he asked, glancing at a table of electrical appliances, all tagged with bright yellow stickers.

"You never know. See that?" Allie asked.

He grimaced at the green-and-purple vase. "That's valuable?"

Allie handled the vase with care. "Makes my heart flutter," she whispered.

"Easily excited, aren't you?"

Laughing, she stepped away. Underneath a table, several stuffed animals peeked out from a carton. Allie weaved around it and another piled with baby clothes. Two chattering housewives elbowed their way past her. Allie drifted to a table of books, then spotted an odd assortment of throwaways on the next table and turned a pewter pitcher upside down. A machine stamp indicated the pitcher had no collector's value.

To pass time, Riley settled beside one table and examined a sabre tossed in a pile with lead pipes and broken hammers. It looked Civil War vintage to him. For two dollars? Looking up, he found Allie staring at him. "Is this…?"

She shook her head.

Shrugging, he scrutinized a coin on another table. Deciding it looked phony, he swung around to see her haggling over the price of the vase with the seller, a fiftyish throwback of the hippie generation with shoulder-length hair and a goatee.

Proudly holding the vase, Allie rejoined Riley by a table a few minutes later. "A girl in school brought one of these to show-and-tell," she said, fingering a Bozo the Clown bank.

"What did you bring?"

"My ballet shoes. I took ballet from the time I was five to the time I was seventeen."

He'd never known that about her.

"That was the big failure in my life. I made a youthful stab at winning a position with a ballet company."

She didn't know real failure, he thought. With every breath he drew for years, in every moment he'd sat alone on a holiday while others gathered with family, he remembered how he'd botched up several lives.

"Are you admiring that?" she asked about the glass-enclosed gun collection.

"Wondering what's hot," he whispered out of the corner of his mouth.

Allie reached up and traced a fingertip down from his cheekbone to his jaw. "Cynic."

"Realist." His frown deepened as he hefted a rifle.

He'd seen one like it before, but at six years old, he hadn't been allowed to touch it. "A twelve-gauge rifle like this one hung in the back of my dad's pickup." Wearing his first pair of cowboy boots, he'd vowed to have a rifle just like that someday. After an accident ended his father's work on the ranch, his dad had gotten rid of the rifle. Thoughts of the rifle had faded, but the boots... The memory crowded Riley's mind. Every time he tugged on a new pair of boots, those moments in his youth when he'd been surrounded by love and laughter teetered near. "Why do people keep so much junk?"

"Didn't you ever have any collections?"

"I had a collection of Captain Marvel comics."

"You should have kept them," Allie said with certainty. "They have value. What happened to them?"

"I've no idea. When I left the house, they were still in boxes under my bed," he said, strolling with her down the alley toward his car. "Some Realtor probably tossed them."

Allie didn't understand. Why hadn't he retrieved them before they'd moved?

"Did you collect anything besides music boxes?"

"Dolls when I was really young. A long time ago, I had a musical ballerina. My father gave it to me when he returned from Amsterdam. I had the other music boxes, but that one was my prize possession for years."

"Because it was from your father?"

She supposed that was true. "It was the last one he gave me. When he left the house that night after he and my mother argued, I took the figurine to bed and prayed he'd come back. He died while away. Angry, I knocked it off the dresser. I didn't want to look at it anymore.''

She'd never told him that story before.

As he opened the door, Allie settled inside. With the shattered glass scattered on the floor of her bedroom, she'd curled up in bed and wept through the night for a father she'd loved, for all the time she hadn't spent with him before his death.

She gave her head an impatient shake, unsure why that moment in her life had come back to her. Was it supposed to remind her of the heartache Devin could endure? Or was it more simple than that? Memories were yesterdays. Perhaps it was time she forgot the past.

After picking up Devin, they found themselves trapped in a rush-hour traffic jam. The car crept slowly forward. The music of Whitney Houston floated from the radio. Allie viewed a family of five in a station wagon a lane over. Did she and Riley and Devin look like a family to others?

"What do you want to eat?" he asked, cutting into her thoughts.

With Devin along, Allie considered simple fare a necessity. "Devin likes Italian food." Her voice softened as she turned to see Devin in the back seat. Lulled by the sound of the engine, he'd fallen asleep. "Forget that idea," she said lightly.

In his rearview mirror, Riley regarded her sleeping son. Their plans had changed.

"You used to like take-out food," Allie commented.

He matched her amused smile. "There's a deli around the corner."

"That's fine."

"Your call. Where do you want to go with it?" He needed to make her choose. "Your mother's house or the apartment?"

Some questions carried more meaning than the words conveyed. The ball was really in her court now. A yes meant more than a relaxing dinner in front of the television set. In that apartment, they'd be captured by memories. "Your place," she answered, before she gave herself too much time to think.

Don't expect too much, Riley cautioned himself. Dinner and a chance to see the apartment might be all she had in mind.

While he dashed from the car to get sandwiches, Allie shifted on the seat and stared at Devin. Deception gnawed at her; cowardliness controlled her. The unknown frightened her. She had no idea how Riley would react to the news about Devin. She only knew she wasn't ready to tell him. What could she say? Oh, by the way, Riley, you're Devin's father. She couldn't blurt out that kind of announcement. Some situations required set-up conversation.

She thought that dilemma the most difficult one she would face. When they reached Riley's apartment, she learned she was wrong.

"I'll carry him up," Riley volunteered, as Allie lifted a sleeping Devin from the car seat.

This was the most difficult moment she'd ever faced, Allie decided, placing Devin in Riley's waiting arms.

She wanted to cry at the sight of her son with his head resting against his father's, his little arms draped over Riley's broad shoulders. With every fiber of her being, she longed for what she knew was impossible.

"Here's the key," he said, dangling his key ring.

The smell of lake air curled around her as she led the way into the building. When she and Riley had gone apartment hunting, she'd been convinced this was where she'd wanted to live with him even before they'd seen the place. The view from his fifth-floor apartment was magnificent, and so was the rent. They'd been satisfied to open a window, hear the sounds of the lake welcoming them awake in the morning.

In the elevator, Allie juggled the diaper bag and a cloth shopping bag of toys, along with a bag containing the corned-beef-on-rye sandwiches. So much had changed since those days.

"You'll have to take him so I can set up this thing." He motioned to the crib-size playard that he'd clutched under his other arm during the ride on the elevator. Silently he eased Devin to her arms when they stepped into the apartment. To his satisfaction, he got the contraption set up quickly. Stepping back, he stared at her cuddling her son. During all the moments he'd remembered her, he'd never visualized her like this. "I'll get plates and napkins," he said, leaving them alone.

Allie assumed she'd always be alone with Devin, but was it her imagination or had Riley held Devin a moment longer than he'd needed to before she'd taken him? In some sense that reached beyond the reality of the moment, was he unconsciously feeling a closeness, a connection with the child who was his flesh and blood?

She would always wonder how he could not see what seemed so visible to her. Except for the dimples so like her own, Devin's smile mirrored his father's. The texture of his hair was so like Riley's that sometimes when she was combing Devin's, she could evoke the feel of Riley's. "I'm not sure what I'm doing," she whispered while lowering Devin into the makeshift crib. "Parents aren't supposed to admit that, but your mommy might be really messing up now." She bent over and kissed him. "He's a wonderful man, Devin. He's gentle and thoughtful and fun. He'd make a wonderful daddy if he wanted to be one."

A big *if,* Allie admitted.

Placing a light blanket on Devin, she turned to join Riley in the kitchen. It was then she looked around her. Everything was as if she'd never left.

The bookcase still bore numerous Robert Ludlum books. How many times had she watched Riley sit for hours engrossed in one of his books? She noticed, too, that one of Stephen King's early books, which she'd brought with her when she'd moved in, still occupied a spot on a bookshelf. All that time she'd been gone, he'd left reminders of her around him, from a cross-stitch pillow on the sofa, a present from

her mother, to the books that individually and together they'd brought home.

From her vantage point in the living room, she saw
that a jade plant she'd started from nothing had developed an inch-thick stem. For someone who forgot
every morning where he'd put his watch the night
before, he'd somehow diligently watered it.

"Something wrong?"

Everything. Her Bauer and Frankenthal porcelains
were gone from a shelf, but nothing else.

"I boxed your statues," Riley said, aware of her
staring at the empty space. "They're in storage."

"You didn't change the apartment?"

"Why would I? Before you moved in, it had the
appeal of a penitentiary cell," he said, leaving her
and disappearing into the bedroom to change his
shirt.

Above the beige sofa with its thin, pale green
stripes hung the eighteenth-century Dutch painting
that she'd found abandoned in a Vermont barn. The
Aubusson rug in dove gray and pale yellow protected
a glossy oak floor. Together they'd spent weeks re-
finishing the floors.

"I did move the highboy," Riley called out from
the bedroom doorway, "and that pine cupboard.
They're in storage, too."

She'd haggled for that pine cupboard at a farm
auction in Wisconsin. Memories held her still. That
night, they'd stayed at the only motel with a vacancy
and had laughed until their sides ached as they were
treated to a vibrating bed. Then, with nothing to do
in the small town, they'd made love all night.

Aware of him still watching her, she ambled into the kitchen. On a far end of the kitchen counter stood a hot pink, porcelain pig with one eye closed in a wink. Riley had thrown pennies into glass dishes to win it for her at a carnival.

"Ugly as ever, isn't it?" Riley asked as she touched it.

"I loved it. It's so atrocious that it's cute."

"That's what you said the first time you saw it."

Memories. The wonderful ones of laughter and loving weren't enough anymore. *Touch me again.* As his eyes met hers, those words lingered on her tongue. She couldn't say them yet. She had to set some boundaries. Last time she'd let herself believe too much in the two of them. This time she wouldn't. They could be lovers, but this time she wouldn't allow herself to fantasize that he loved her.

Gathering her thoughts, she strode back to the living room, stopping at the window. "I told myself I didn't feel the same for you anymore." She could see a portion of the lake, of the swells lapping at the shoreline. Turning, she leaned against a wall. "That was a lie." That he remained silent unnerved her. "You aren't saying anything."

"I didn't think you were finished." His eyes never leaving hers, he moved near. Once he touched her, felt her willingness, he wouldn't stop. "Are you?"

"No, I'm not." Caressingly, she brushed her fingers across the edge of a mahogany end table that he'd driven eighty miles, across the Wisconsin state line, to get for her, because she'd wanted it. "I know you don't want any long-term relationship."

She moved again, avoided looking at him, fearful that she wouldn't say the necessary words. "I know you don't want anyone permanent in your life. You don't want anyone." It hurt to say even those words. "And we'll complicate each other's lives." There was more to consider than just them. Too much more, Allie thought. There was a child who needed a father's love, a wonderful little boy who'd give Riley more than he'd ever get from anyone else. He'd love him if Riley would let him—with no conditions. Devin would make him laugh and smile when he felt lousy. He'd call him Daddy and make it sound like the most wonderful word in the world.

In her clumsy way, she was working toward telling him about Devin. She wanted to tell him about all that, about all the nights she'd wept for them. She really did, but she said nothing.

Behind him the phone rang, slicing through the silence surrounding them. For a long second, Allie stood still. He wasn't moving, either. "Are you going to answer it?" she asked, sweeping a hand toward the phone.

Answering a telephone was the last thing on his mind. "Let it ring."

She knew that was impossible for her. "You don't expect me to ignore a ringing phone, do you?"

He knew she couldn't and felt almost relief. He had no business touching her, doing this to her again. "Still can't do it?"

"Still can't," she admitted. He used to tease her about jumping over furniture to answer a ringing phone.

"Okay, we'll compromise." Moving away took effort. "*You* pick it up, but tell the person that I'm not here. That way you get to satisfy your curiosity and I don't have to talk to anyone." He looked away from the button on her blouse tempting him to open it. "I'll get those plates."

So close. They'd been so close. She turned to the telephone with a frown. Had it rung at that moment like some signal, to stop her before they were tangled in each other's life?

Snatching up the receiver, she offered a greeting. As she listened to the operator, doing what Riley had requested suddenly seemed impossible. "Riley, it's a collect call. From Texas."

He reappeared in the kitchen doorway, frowning. What the hell was going on in his sister's life now? "I'm not here," he said, even though Allie held the receiver toward him, expecting him to take it.

"You're not..." Allie watched him whip away. Dumbfounded, she delivered a message to the operator. Wasn't his sister still in Texas? Why wouldn't he talk to her? Setting the receiver back in its cradle, Allie wanted to ask questions. It was then she saw the unopened, wrinkled envelope.

The postmark caught her eye—Texas. Another reminder, a simple one like the phone call, sent doubts soaring within her. Maybe it was a mistake to have come here. Nothing had changed, not really. Riley kept a part of himself from her, always would.

With plates in hand, he strolled back into the room. Her mood had changed. She stood tense, her back straight, her eyes riveted to the table. He damned the phone call, then realized the letter had helped spoil the mood. "Spit it out. What do you want to say?"

She released a brief, dismissive laugh in the manner of someone trying to backpedal conversation and play a scene differently. "There is a disadvantage to knowing each other too well, isn't there?"

Closely he studied her. He didn't buy her casual act. "There are advantages to it, too. Are you going to be honest?"

It occurred to her that the next moment might wipe away their last chance. "Are you?"

His eyes narrowed with questions. "What are you getting at?"

"You don't want to know."

"You never used to play games."

She faced him with a challenge gleaming in her eyes. "Why didn't you take the phone call or open the letter?" Oh, why was she doing this? she wondered immediately. "Never mind," she said with disgust at herself. She'd eat dinner with him and leave before she made a real mess of everything.

He set the plates on the coffee table. "Do you know how often you said that to me and meant just the opposite?"

"If you want, I'll leave," she said, because nothing would be right now.

"You did that once to me already."

"I wasn't the one who left first. Who ended everything? You did." Anger resurrected the hurt she'd felt and thought she'd buried. "You were leaving for Texas without an explanation."

"That's history."

"History repeats itself," Allie countered. "Before you left, you told me you were going. Nothing else. For that matter, you've never talked about your family. You breezed over details."

"I told you what was important," he said, in a tone that allowed for no opposition.

Disbelief settled on her face. "You still don't understand, do you?" she said rather than asked.

"Why are you pushing this now?"

Why was she? Was it because she knew if she was with him again she'd be as close to opening her heart to him as she'd been before? "Because it makes me realize that I wasn't wrong to leave." The words were hurtful, but protective instincts insisted on them. "I wanted to know about you. I cared…" She paused and admitted, "I loved you. I wanted to know what was wrong, and you wouldn't tell me. About you. Your family. The people you love."

There was no one he could let himself love, not even her. "What's to know?" Annoyance with her persistence tightened his jaw. "At sixteen I moved around a lot."

When he'd told her that before, she'd thought it hadn't made sense. It couldn't have been so simple. "You couldn't have. You had a younger brother and sister."

The dark eyes he'd longed to see for so long never wavered with their curiosity and challenge. If he told her, he'd open himself to all that misery again. Keeping secrets from her had never been his plan. He'd simply shoved that time in his life to some distant part of his mind, not wanting to remember emotions that had been so unbearable he'd wept with them.

Allie watched his chest rise and fall heavily, as if he was laboring for breath. Regret closed in on her for the pain she sensed she was reviving in him, but if she backed off, anything possible between them would flutter away.

"You need to know?" he asked, so quietly she strained to hear him.

"This isn't for me," Allie answered softly.

He steeled himself to the appeal in her eyes and voice. "Saving me from myself?"

"Do you need saving?"

He ran a hand across his face, feeling weary of skirting her persistence. "I lost them."

"Lost? Lost who?" Allie asked, puzzled.

"First my brother, then my sister."

His words made no sense to her. "But you know where your sister is."

"Now. But I didn't for a long time." He moved across the room, not wanting Allie's touch, anything too gentle. "I knew what would happen when authorities learned that our parents had died. I packed some clothes, and I kept moving them around, trying to dodge the social services people so they wouldn't separate us."

Allie stared at his profile, at the tightening of his jaw. "What do you mean, you moved around?"

"We slept in the car. We washed up at gas-station rest rooms. Every morning I'd drive them to school. Then I'd pick them up, and we did the same damn thing again the next day."

She looked beyond his words. They'd lived as if homeless. Three children.

"One day I came for my brother after school. He wasn't there."

Tilting her head, Allie could see the pain in Riley's eyes.

"They took him out of school. Screaming and kicking, I understand. He was seven. I never saw him again."

With a sharp breath, she sat on the sofa, feeling as if someone had knocked the air from her. She hadn't expected this. Now that he'd told her, she didn't know what to say.

As if she wasn't there, he spoke quietly. "My sister was eleven. If it happened to him, I figured it would happen to her. I knew my brother was already caught in the system. I couldn't find him, so I decided to leave Wyoming with her, keep hopping around so no one could find us. That was my plan."

He sat in a chair across from her, leaning forward, resting his elbows on his knees. Head bent, he stared at the floor. "I'd been working in a gas station while they were at school. I'd known a secret hiding place where my mother stashed some money. I made a mistake. I drove to the house. It had only been two weeks since my parents died. I figured everything would still be there."

He'd had no time to mourn, Allie realized. He'd had no one to help him, to reassure him.

"I left Cindy in the car and went in the house. Some neighbor, some well-meaning do-gooder, called the cops. They came and picked up both of us. We were dragged off to social services.''

Seconds passed, silent seconds. He sat so still for so long that Allie was afraid for him. ''Riley?''

He gave a shake of his head, as if pulling himself back from some distant place. ''I was there two days, then ran. I ran like hell to get away.''

Allie shivered, chilled by his calm, flat tone.

''I had no idea where she was. And I couldn't do anything about that.''

She agonized for the grief he concealed within him—and the guilt. Heavy, unbearable guilt; guilt that wasn't his burden to carry.

''For the next two years, I wandered. I got jobs here and there, enough to eat. I never stayed in one place too long. If I did, they'd find me. So I kept moving until I turned eighteen.''

And never connected with anyone, Allie thought sadly. Never committed to anything for years. The pressure behind her eyes grew heavier. Lowering her head, she stared at the tips of her sneakers. Sadness for him overwhelmed her. When she'd first met him, she'd seen that smile, had loved his lighthearted nature, the way he viewed life as if he didn't have a care in the world. He hid so much sadness, so much emptiness so well. Moving close, she knelt before him and touched his hand.

Pure willpower kept him from tensing. For over a decade he'd learned that if he didn't soften, if he didn't give in to all the pain that often seemed a breath away, he wouldn't crumble. ''It happened a long time ago,'' he insisted, fighting the pressure crowding his throat and chest.

She sensed what he was denying. To him, those difficult days had happened yesterday. ''I'm sorry.''

''So am I,'' he said emotionlessly. ''I'm sorry for all that I couldn't do.''

She wanted to wrap her arms around him. ''How could you expect so much from a sixteen-year-old boy?'' she asked, pressing her forehead to his.

How could he not? He was all they'd had. ''They expected me to protect them, and I couldn't,'' he said in a low voice, hating to hear those words, ones he'd never said to anyone before.

Allie took a deep breath. He'd let her in, but he already regretted it. If he closed himself up now, he'd never let her reach out to him again. She took a chance and slipped her arms around his waist, felt him stiffen. ''Let me hold you.'' Nothing felt steady. Her heart hammered so fast she'd thought it would burst through her chest. ''Make love with me. That's why I came tonight.''

He caught a handful of hair and gently drew it back to force her eyes to meet his, wanting to see the truth in them. ''Did you?'' Why was she coming to him in the wake of sympathy? He wanted her to ache for him, not pity him.

Tension smoldered in the air.

Slowly he slipped his fingers through her hair. ''I should tell you to leave.'' His gaze followed the creamy flesh that narrowed at her throat and disappeared under the soft cloth of her blouse. ''We both know I won't give you what you want.''

No, no promises would be made. She expected none. But she wanted to be with him.

He felt the heat of her hands on his back. He should stop, for her sake. She could rattle off words about no commitment, but he knew her. She was a bundle of emotion; she led with her heart. And if she allowed him to, he'd break it again.

His lips skimmed along her cheek to her ear. He couldn't push her away. He'd die if he had to.

Chapter Eight

Allie's blood pounded in her ears, drowning out the low wail of a love song by Garth Brooks drifting from the radio. She wouldn't have let Riley push her away this time. Tonight, he'd given her something he'd offered to no one else. He'd shared with her, and by doing so, he'd brought them back together again. There was more to say, but not now. Too many feelings she'd smothered since she'd left him seemed close at hand, and all she wanted was within her grasp.

As she raised her parted lips, roughly his mouth moved over hers. Her taste filled him with the same kind of longing as before. "I never stopped thinking about you."

Her eyes on his, she began unbuttoning his shirt. He would hurt her again, though not intentionally, but neither the past nor the future seemed important right now. As he peeled off his shirt, her lips clung to his.

Desire for her soft flesh taunted him. "I always thought your skin was softer than velvet," he murmured, his fingertips grazing her shoulder as he lifted her blouse from it. With tenderness, he slid the straps of her camisole off her shoulders, let the silk slither over her breasts.

A fire burned in his lungs. What he'd felt before didn't compare to this. She was his passion, his need. Only she would ever satisfy his hunger. He'd begun a pursuit, planning a few quick dates to get her out of his system. Now he wondered if he'd ever be able to walk away. When he lowered her to the sofa, he didn't want to think about more than that. With hands not quite steady, he tugged at her jeans, rolled her panties down her hips. He fought a need to rush her, wanted to give her all he could, make her regret leaving. He wanted to leave her mindless.

But already she was shattering his senses, her mouth hot and moist on his, her hand rubbing against him. The snap on his jeans popped. Together they worked to rid him of denim. A shudder rippled through him. He thought he had control, but at her stroking, he hissed out a breath. Control wouldn't be his for long.

Frantic for his taste, Allie framed his face with her hands. He murmured her name, his hands roaming over her, his lips caressing her shoulder. Then his mouth captured hers again. This time the pressure was gentle, almost reverent, making her feel treasured. At that moment, she thought she'd die without his touch. At that moment, she knew she was lost.

Her heart leading her, she ran trembling hands down the muscles of his back and upper arms to savor the feel of his flesh, heating now. One kiss blended into another, deepening, growing more insistent, more demanding. Then his mouth left hers. Hands that promised to bring her to a feverish pitch glided across her breasts, down her belly.

The bond that had begun years ago linked them again. A flood of wanting flowed over her until she couldn't get enough of him. With eyes half-closed, she trembled as his tongue played across her flesh to the warmth between her thighs and drove into her. Sensation after sensation rippled through her, courtesy of his fingers, his mouth, his tongue. Arching toward him, her body heated to a fever pitch. Nothing was enough. There was only the needs of the flesh.

Greedy, she wanted more and wrapped her legs around his back. She called out his name and caught his hair in her fingers to bring him closer. There was no pause. He played with and stroked her as if determined to make her never forget the experience. Her world tilted and, breathless, she cried out. A shift in movement; more madness and craving. Then he lowered himself to her.

When he slipped inside her, she drew him even deeper, coaxing him to lead her, wanting him to fill her. They moved hard against each other, their bodies each pounding to meet its own fierce demand, their hunger driving them to a mindless place of swirling sensations. Softly he spoke, murmuring her name, muttering unintelligible words. She didn't need whispers. Shuddering again, she was his. She had always been his.

Only the flickering lights of candles illuminated the room. Content, Allie nuzzled against him for another moment. She yearned for it to last forever.

Riley doubted he could move even if he wanted to. For a long moment, he lay there struggling to breathe and waiting for his heart to slow its beat. She brushed her fingers down his back and he felt heat flowing through his body. She'd given him more than he'd anticipated, more than he'd ever recalled. Even as his trembling muscles steadied, the sweet, dark longing to taste and caress her spiraled through him once more.

Rolling her with him, he held her tight. A greedy need to see her eyes filled him. He stared into them, dark and warm and loving, her face bathed in the moist warmth of their lovemaking. He skimmed his fingers, featherlight, along her rib cage. "Any regrets?"

She had only one now. She wished he'd known the truth about Devin. But too much emotion already electrified the air. If she told him about Devin now, the trust gained would be snatched away. "Do you?"

"Only that you weren't here with me sooner," he murmured against her neck. "You make me weak." And strong. An amazing paradox.

"Let me try again."

Slowly, tantalizingly, she stroked her fingers down

his chest. A silver sheen of moonlight played over her bare skin as they fluttered lower. One simple caress snatched the air from his lungs.

Shifting, she got to her knees, her palms resting on his belly. In the shadowed light, he saw her smile before she bent her head. Strands of her hair brushed the tops of his thighs and he thought he might go mad. Effortlessly she detonated a fire within him. She made him tremble. Then a fierce wave of sensation rushed through him. He closed his eyes, no longer able to think.

With the gray softness of dawn, Allie remained still, her head resting on Riley's chest. Through the doorway, she saw the chair in the living room where he'd tossed her camisole. She needed to get up before Devin woke and burst into tears because of his strange surroundings.

His eyes closed, Riley stroked her hip slowly, sensuously. He knew that in minutes she would bound from the bed they'd moved to during the night. He preferred easing his way off the mattress. He preferred neither of them moving at all this morning. "Janet won't blink twice if you're not there right away. She knows you're with me."

"But I need to make breakfast for Devin." Allie inched away from Riley before his caress grew more seductive. "I know you," she said, stepping out of the room to retrieve her clothes. "There's no milk, no cereal." Head bent, she returned to the bedroom and lounged against the edge of the dresser to button her blouse. "There's nothing to feed him here."

Reluctantly Riley swung his legs out of the bed. He couldn't argue with her. He had beer, cheese, crackers—not exactly a breakfast fit for a child. "Why don't you leave his crib here?"

Allie looked up to see him yanking on his jeans. Would he feel as generous with his space if he knew how much of it one little boy, this little boy, could take up in his life? "Are you thinking ahead?"

"Might as well leave it here." Riley snatched up his T-shirt and pulled it over his head. He had no disillusions, but what had been between them left unfinished business. He'd discovered she could still be his. He'd learned, too, that she could still enchant him without doing a thing. "You might get tired and want to sleep here again."

At his muffled words, Allie waited until his head popped through the shirt opening. "Sleep?"

"Whatever." Letting her leave was proving difficult. Last night had spun a web of intimacy over them, like the one that had captured and bound them together night after night years ago. Until he'd held her body close, naked and damp with desire, he'd forgotten how just having her near made him feel different. Complete. "Come back after work. We'll go to the movies tonight. We might find a drive-in."

Allie paused in slipping on her shoes. "I haven't been to a drive-in since I was seventeen."

"Great place to make moves on a girl."

She arched a brow at him. "You know this from personal experience?"

"The first time I went to one I was older than you were your last time." He dropped to the edge of the bed and tugged on one boot then the other. "Twenty-one. I thought I owned the world. I'd just joined the police force, bought my first car."

"And you wanted to show it off?"

"She was a beauty."

"The car or the girl?"

He stood and tugged Allie close. "The car. But now that I think about it, so was the girl."

Tilting her head back, she kissed a corner of his mouth. "Was she impressed with your car?"

"My moves," he said, running his hand over her backside.

She released a husky laugh. "So modest."

"I'll even provide dinner tonight," he whispered, slipping fingers into the softness of her hair.

"Should I ask what a man who brings pizza for breakfast will give me for dinner?"

"Pancakes," he said, and muffled her laughter with a kiss.

Riley abandoned any thought of going back home to sleep. How had he survived without her? he wondered. It was a thought he wanted to block and couldn't. He knew they hadn't discussed the reality of their relationship. She no longer wanted to live her life from one day to the next, taking off on weekend ski trips or sailing Lake Michigan all night, and then dashing from his boat to work. She was different; he wasn't.

He missed the Allie who'd left two years ago, the one who rushed through grocery stores while he dawdled behind her reading labels, the one who'd loved walking in the rain, who'd argue the benefits of healthier foods while licking at an ice-cream cone.

Maybe if he had a soul mate to pour thoughts out to, he'd understand better why everything had changed. But he had no one. When Allie had left, he'd told his partner. What he hadn't shared with Nick were the sleepless nights. No one knew how often he'd stopped dead in his tracks, catching his breath when he'd caught a glimpse of red hair beneath bright sunlight and had believed he'd seen her. He'd never shared the sense of emptiness, of loneliness that had burrowed within him. He'd never told anyone, not even her, that she was the one person he loved.

Feeling like a teenager, Allie sneaked quietly into her mother's house and began making Devin's breakfast. She rode an emotional seesaw, being happier than she'd been during the past two years, yet badgered by guilt. She couldn't shut out doubts that she'd made a mistake two years ago, that her decision to leave without telling Riley had deprived Devin and Riley of each other. She couldn't stop worrying. What if Riley wanted Devin, hated her for keeping his son from him?

"Oh, you two got home," her mother said too brightly as she strode into the kitchen.

Allie expected questions.

"Did you have a good time?"

That wasn't what she wanted to know. "Yes, we did."

With healthy gusto, Devin dug his spoon into the bowl of oatmeal Allie set before him.

Her mother paused in pouring coffee for herself. "Since you didn't come home, I thought you might have fallen asleep there."

Allie laughed at her mother's reminder of an excuse she'd given for coming home after curfew when she was seventeen. "I told you. Nothing happened that night. Chad Stewart didn't even kiss me. That's why we fell asleep. We were both bored."

"Oh, yes, now I remember," her mother's voice teased.

"You still don't believe me?"

"I believe you. So nothing happened last night, either?"

"Mother, I don't ask you about your sex life, do I?"

"Of course not. Mine's practically nil right now," she said with a sigh of disgust. "But yours might be rather interesting."

Before leaving for the store, Allie hugged Devin so tightly he squirmed in her arms. Last night Riley had opened to her a part of his life she'd never known about. He'd taken a giant step when he'd finally told her about the days with his brother and sister. Trust. He'd given her the gift of trust, sharing some of the pain. He understood secrets; he kept them himself. Somehow she would explain why she'd kept hers.

Carol's mumbling greeted Allie when she stepped into the shop. "Is something wrong?"

"Men are what's wrong with this world."

Allie laughed as Carol divulged a story about her ex-husband's escapade with a blond bimbo strip-teaser whose specialty was bird feathers strategically placed. "The man is tasteless. And that's what led to the divorce."

"But he wants you back now?"

"He does," Carol said, looking pleased.

Smiling, Allie returned to the main portion of the shop to greet a customer. Instead a florist delivery man grinned at her.

"Allison Harrigan?" he asked, checking his clipboard.

She nodded and accepted the package he gave her. Inside was a small green plant in no ordinary porcelain planter. This one was a green-and-black frog.

Carol smirked. "That's cute." She tipped her head to draw Allie's attention. "There's a reason for that, isn't there?"

"I collect animals, mostly cheap figurines—cows and ducks—and frogs." This was more than a romantic gesture. It was meant to touch her. Riley always had. "So back to your problem. You're still in love with your ex?"

"Ridiculously." Carol kept staring at the frog.

"Why don't you sit down and talk about everything?" Maybe if you talk..." Allie paused. Who was she to give such advice?

"It seems dumb not to, doesn't it?" Carol agreed. "Since I'm miserable without him."

"It doesn't make sense for you to keep fighting

what you want...." Her voice trailed off with those words. Wasn't she doing the same?

"I can't give in so easily. How do I know he's not still thinking with what's below his belt?"

"Man's downfall." A woman's, too, sometimes, Allie reflected. "Lust," she said firmly in response to Carol's questioning look.

"Ah, you, too?" Carol paused in stroking a feather duster down the legs of a Hepplewhite chair.

With plans to take the frog and plant home, Allie set it on a shelf behind the counter.

"We have an advantage, you know." Carol touched a leaf of the plant. "We know what they like. We could enjoy driving them crazy to have us."

Allie laughed. That was advice she might take. "Old movies," she mumbled to herself. They'd watched them often enough while in bed. Riley loved watching them. An idea taking form, she grinned while she reached for the telephone.

Riley scowled at his watch. Waiting for an autopsy report gave him too much time to think.

He yanked the telephone book out from under his desk and skimmed a finger down the list of antique shops for the number for Cherished Treasures.

No hazy memories had drawn Allie and him back together; vivid, clear-cut moments had done it. But what had been only skimmed the surface. He thought it maddening that he could want her more now than he had before, that what he felt now could reach so deeply within him.

His hand on the receiver, he nearly jumped as the

phone rang. With a quick glance around him, he assured himself no one had seen his reaction. He'd be razzed for days about acting so spooked. "Garrison, homicide," he answered impatiently.

"Hi. The frog is adorable." He heard the smile in her voice.

"I'm glad you liked it."

"You knew I would." Allie rotated a pen in her hand. "I had another reason for calling."

"You want to know what I'm making for dinner."

Her laugh rippled through the phone to him. "No, I'll take my chances. I called to see if you wanted to skip the drive-in. There's a great movie on television tonight."

"Are you asking me for a date?" he teased.

"No, you asked me this morning."

"Guess I did."

"I'm just changing plans."

No amount of reasoning overshadowed the pleasure coursing through him. "Any reason for that?"

"It's a great movie."

"That's the only reason?"

She didn't reply to that, but he could hear a smile in her voice when she said, "I didn't notice this morning. Do you still have a television in the bedroom?"

"Still have it."

"Perfect. See ya."

For a long moment after he heard the click signaling she'd hung up, he held the phone. Only when he placed the receiver back in its cradle did he finally release a long, not-too-steady breath. Then he laughed.

She missed him, Allie realized, catching herself clock watching several times that day. If she couldn't be away from him for a few hours without such feelings, what kind of emotional morass would she endure when it was over again?

That question bothered her more than she liked.

That evening when she rang his doorbell, she tried to remember that this time wasn't the same. He'd opened himself to her. And once she told him about Devin, there would be no secrets. She'd watched them together. Riley genuinely liked Devin already. Surely, once he knew Devin was his son, he would feel even more, and eventually he would love him like he should.

"I thought you'd never get here," he said, opening the door.

Laughing, she stepped into his arms. What she yearned for was a possibility, a very real one, she decided. With a long sigh, she shut her eyes and coiled her arms around his neck. How right it always felt to be in his embrace.

"You'd better come in," he whispered against her hair. All day he'd dealt with impatience to see her again. "I'm feeling an uncontrollable urge to make love to you in the hallway." She laughed, but he had never been more serious in his life. Drawing back, he grabbed her hands, pulled her in and kicked the door shut.

Allie felt giddy with happiness. "Very macho," she teased.

"You haven't seen anything yet." He caught her to him, stirring another laugh from her.

"Where's Devin?"

"My mother volunteered to watch him." Quieting, she sniffed exaggeratedly. "You cooked?" Turning her face toward the kitchen, she sniffed again, trying to zero in on the aroma. It was spicy. "Spaghetti?"

"Hmm," he murmured against her ear. The scent of her fragrance enticed him more. "Syrup is messy in bed."

Leaning back against his arm at her waist, she swept a look around the room. He'd tried not to overdo the romance thing some women expected. A bottle of wine chilled in the refrigerator; a few candles on the coffee table flickered. He'd lowered the lights only a notch.

"Everything looks nice."

A little embarrassed, he simply nodded. "Come on into the kitchen," he said, certain he'd better rescue their dinner before he completely forgot about it. "How was your day?" he asked with a backward glance.

"Decent sales." He looked wonderful and sexy standing at the stove, stirring spaghetti sauce. Sun-bleached hair, slightly disarrayed from the rake of his fingers, tempted her touch. Her eyes swept down to his bare feet. Seeing him like this brought back memories of all the times he'd come in the door whistling, always whistling, and immediately tugged off his boots. He always padded barefoot around the apartment. She'd once suggested that he buy sneakers. He'd curled his lip at the idea, telling her no man from Wyoming wore sneakers. She'd laughed with him before he'd tumbled her to the floor, before his mouth and hands had driven her senseless.

"No ogre brother-in-law snapping at your heels?"

"No." Allie eyed the newspaper Riley had left open on the kitchen table. "He's probably in his dungeon planning my next torture."

She spoke lightly, but Riley heard an edge of uneasiness in her voice. "There's nothing he can do to you." He wouldn't let him.

"No, there isn't. But you know me." Too well for her to fool him. "My favorite pastime is worrying about what might happen." Not wanting to let Jason spoil their evening, she pointed a finger at a theater listing. "This one is supposed to be good."

Over her shoulder, he squinted at the newspaper. "I've seen it. It's dumb. And didn't you say we were staying in?"

Unable to resist, she moved to stand beside him at the stove and rested a hand on the nape of his neck. "Why is it dumb?"

He angled his face toward her. "She commits suicide at the end, stabbing herself because some guy disgraced her."

"Not realistic enough for you?" she asked with a laugh.

"Hardly." He kissed the side of her neck. "More likely she'd do him in instead."

"And you'd have another homicide," she said,

scrunching her neck as his tongue teasingly grazed it.

"She'd get caught," he murmured, her sigh encouraging him.

Feeling weak, she nearly closed her eyes.

"So what's this movie that's so great on television?" he asked. If the evening went as he planned, he doubted they'd see more than the opening credits.

Allie sensed a night of teasing as he stepped back toward the stove. "A great suspense flick," she assured him. *"Gaslight."*

"Know what year it was made?" he asked, handing her a loaf of crusty bread to cut.

"That's easy to answer." Allie located a knife and sliced quickly. "Nineteen forty-four." She loved this game with him. They'd learned early in their relationship that they both considered themselves movie buffs. "Who starred in it besides Charles Boyer, Ingrid Bergman and Joseph Cotten?" she asked, smiling back at him.

His eyes sparkled with humor. "Big star?"

"Yes." She chomped on a piece of the bread. "I'll give you a clue."

"Don't bother," he said, as if insulted she'd suggest such a thing.

"Let me help. Big television star."

His brows furrowed in concentration.

"Come on, Garrison." With a fingertip she traced the faint line between his brows. "You always claimed you're more of a movie expert than I am."

He accepted her teasing challenge without hesitation. Though she'd played this game of movie trivia like an expert often enough, he'd sat alone too many nights in a dumpy room not fit for anyone, watching a secondhand television that he'd bought with his first paycheck from the police force. In the middle of the night, entertaining fare meant B movies and classic oldies. He watched because he couldn't sleep.

"Stumped?"

"Surely you jest!" Giving her a devilish grin, he caught her at the waist and dropped to a chair with her on his lap. "But is there a reward for this?"

Laughter dancing in her eyes, Allie coiled an arm around his neck and sent him a seductive look. "Whether you answer or not, you get one."

Grinning, he nibbled at a corner of her mouth. "I like the way you think."

Allie read the meaning behind the gleam in his eyes. "Not hungry?"

"Are you?"

"Of course, I am," she said, reaching behind them to turn off the burner. "You never answered my question." Head bent, she fingered and undid one button on his shirt, then the next.

The scent of her fragrance enticing him, he turned his attentions to her throat. "Angela Lansbury."

"You win." She sighed, her stomach muscles tightening in response to his lips' descent. Like a butterfly's caress, they traced her collarbone.

"Did you tell Janet you'd be staying?"

Twisting from him, she stretched for her shoulder bag and slowly withdrew a black nightie.

"Guess you did," he murmured against her mouth.

Chapter Nine

Like every other morning during the past week, Allie left Riley's apartment before dawn and rushed home before Devin awakened. In her room at her mother's, she pulled off the towel she'd wrapped around herself after a shower. Sunshine warmed the room as she slipped on her bra and panties, then clothes for work.

The aroma of bacon sizzling in a frying pan drifted through the hallway to the bedroom. Allie guessed her mother was happily preparing another lumberjack breakfast, which she'd refuse. Persistence was her mother's best trait and often her worst. So was honesty. Allie had always believed she'd inherited that trait. Then, when tested, she'd learned how easily she took to deception. An honest woman would have told Riley the truth about Devin by now.

Tucking her T-shirt into her jeans, she checked on Devin before she left for the shop. It wasn't that she was dishonest, she tried to assure herself. Since that first night with Riley, she'd begun to believe he might offer more this time. Wishful thinking maybe. But she thought it best that Riley really care about Devin before she told him the truth.

Best for whom? a nagging little voice countered.

For everyone. Riley would feel something for his son, which was what she wanted for Devin. And she'd...well, she wouldn't have to tell him yet, and possibly rip away the happiness she'd found.

It amazed her how much her life had changed in such a short time. A month, a few weeks ago, she'd thought Riley would never be a part of her and Devin's life, and suddenly she couldn't imagine him not being near.

Personally, so much had changed, as had another facet of her life. A sense of sadness swept over her whenever she thought about giving up the store. If Jason hadn't demanded immediate payment on the loan, she'd keep it. She could bring Devin to work with her, and eventually, if successful, pick and choose her work hours so they'd have more time together.

It occurred to her that afternoon, when she was standing in the storeroom of her shop, how easily that goal had been swept away. One IOU threatened to wipe out her savings. For days, she'd sorted through invoices and printouts of ledgers to make sense of the finances at Cherished Treasures. A terrible businessman, Mitch had revealed a careless manner in recording accounts and documenting inventory.

For a moment she viewed a wall of unopened crates, then bent over to shove at a steamer trunk, the smallest of several big pieces blocking her path to the crates. What had possessed Mitch to purchase so much when the business was in the red? And why had he failed to show so little enthusiasm for the items that he'd never checked them, not even for shipping damage? She pushed the trunk forward only a few inches, then straightened, disgusted.

"Is that your way of building muscles?" Riley grinned at her when she whirled around with a startled look.

As swiftly as her heart had quickened, it slowed to a normal beat. "You...!" The teasing reprimand remained unsaid.

"Allie!" Carol called from the other room, popping into the storeroom doorway a second later. She opened her mouth to speak, but words weren't necessary.

Jason stormed past her. "What do you think you're doing?" he bellowed.

"Excuse me." Allie took one long, calming breath. "What are you talking about?"

"I learned this morning that you're having a sale here, selling the inventory."

"That's right. I have bills to pay," she reminded him unnecessarily.

"You have no right to sell anything here. This is mine."

Allie felt her back straighten instinctively. "No,

it's mine.'' She studied him for a moment. ''Did you think that I'd be overwhelmed by the problems facing me, especially the one you dropped in my lap, and would throw my hands up in the air like some insipid woman incapable of handling anything too stressful?''

Despite an urge to rush to her rescue, Riley kept his feet planted. Allison Harrigan never would be a damsel in distress. He made himself turn away, distance himself from their conversation.

''I have no intention of walking away from everything here so you can have it all,'' Allie said softly, not wanting customers in the other rooms to overhear. Though seething, she delivered a humorless smile. ''This is mine, Jason.'' He'd never intimidated her before. She didn't plan to let him start now. ''I'll do whatever I want with it.''

Fury tensed his features. ''We'll see about that,'' he said through clenched teeth before he whipped away, storming past customers to reach the exit.

Allie held firm until she heard the slam of the door. A slow count to ten helped. His threat didn't faze her. Legally he couldn't stop her from selling the inventory, but he sure knew the right buttons to push to unsettle her.

''Guess you told him, huh?''

Allie heard admiration in Riley's voice. No way would she let him know how much she was shaking within. Not wanting to think, much less talk about Jason, she took control of the conversation. ''Didn't you say Nick was due back today?''

''The honeymoon is over.'' Actually, his partner

had sauntered in, looking like a blissful husband who'd obviously spent more time in the stateroom with Ann than on the deck of that cruise ship.

"Did they have a wonderful time?"

"Guess so." Riley eyed the doughnuts on the counter in the kitchen. "He keeps grinning like he's got a secret."

He does, Allie reflected. It's called love. "Want coffee?" She waited only for his nod, then pivoted toward the coffee brewer. Along with the coffee cup, she set a napkin on the table for him.

"Thanks." She always insisted that he hid emotions, but he thought she was doing an admirable job of it herself. Straddling a chair, he watched her set one of the doughnuts before him. "Nick and Ann want us over for dinner one night."

Us. Who'd decided they were an "us"? Nick? Or had Riley indicated they'd become a couple again?

He picked up the doughnut between his thumb and index finger. "What do you say?"

Allie chose a chocolate-covered doughnut for herself and took a huge bite.

"I thought you'd like to get to know her better."

Savoring the doughnut, she nodded.

His eyes narrowing, he studied her for a moment. "Are you done chewing?"

"All done," she said after a swallow.

"Want to do that?"

"I'd love to," she said, liking the "us" part.

"So what else can I do here?" he asked, with a sweep of his arm toward her shop.

"You keep saying that and I'll volunteer you to play furniture mover again."

"I offered, didn't I?"

"You're serious?"

He gave her his best frown for questioning his offer. "What's first?"

"That is." She pointed to a New England sawbuck table and felt a laugh bubble in her throat at his groan.

While he wrestled the table across the wood floor, Allie scanned the address on one of the crates, then began prying it open with a crowbar.

"I'll do that." Gently Riley shoved her aside with his hip.

Allie waited while he fiercely yanked at the metal clips that fastened the top of the crate. As soon as he stepped back, she shoved aside packing material. The crate contained a three-foot-high, smiling Buddha painted a deep rich Chinese red. "Why in the world would he have purchased that?"

"These aren't your purchases?"

"No, Mitch bought these," she answered, motioning toward the other crates. "What do you imagine he was thinking when he bought this?"

If the rest of the crates contained similar junk, Riley thought the answer was obvious. "He liked throwing away money."

Slowly Allie raised her head. Too much truth existed in his flippant comment. "I wonder," she murmured. "I wonder if that was his plan."

"I don't understand."

She saw his puzzled look. "The dates on these

shipments were around the time Mitch was drinking heavily. I think—I always thought—that that was his way of rebelling against Jason."

"That doesn't make sense to me. We're talking about two grown men." Riley settled on one of the crates. "One doesn't rebel against the other. If he doesn't like something, he ignores the other person or tells him to go to hell."

"In a way," she said, dropping onto one of the crates beside him, "he did that when he married me. Jason didn't approve of me. Looking back, I believe that's why Mitch wanted to marry me."

"What about love?"

Odd that he'd consider love important, she mused. "He fooled himself into believing he loved me." She rose to open another crate. "Already in debt, did he spend money just to hurt Jason, to lose part of the family business?"

Her husband sounded weak to Riley. He couldn't fathom allowing anyone that kind of control over him.

Allie shook her head in disbelief as she unpacked a Tibetan parasol, a Nippon vase, a duck-head walking cane and several foreign, inexpensive knick-knacks. "If the rest of the crates hold nothing more valuable, I'll be lucky to get two hundred dollars for all of it."

Gently Riley curled a hand over her shoulder to draw her back against him. Life was throwing her a lot of curves.

Sighing, Allie took the crowbar from him and set it down. Jason never failed to emotionally exhaust her. "I'm going to open the rest of the crates to-morrow."

He sensed her need for an escape from her own thoughts. After a bad day in homicide, he'd look for a sanctuary from everything, a place to refocus until some peace of mind grabbed hold. And he always went to the same place to find it. "Is Devin too young for us to take on the sailboat? I know where I can get a kid's life jacket."

That he'd asked to take Devin with them had to mean something, didn't it? "No, he's not too young."

"Then let's go."

Riley had thought he'd made the suggestion because he wanted to give her the sunlight, the warmth, the wind—let it all take her away from the rest of the world, away from her own thoughts.

The moment he turned onto Lake Shore Drive and the smell of the lake grew stronger, he realized why he'd really brought her sailing. Whatever might or might not happen between him and Allie, he'd wanted to see her on the boat again.

So she could climb aboard, he reached out and, with no hesitation, took Devin from her. A warm breeze whirled around them, tousling their hair. Allie felt a dull pang seeing them so close. Holding Devin in one arm, Riley offered her a hand. His palm met hers, its roughness so in opposition to the gentleness of his embrace of Devin. That little voice inside her head nagged at her again. No more hedging. Whatever the consequences, she would face them. Tonight she would tell him.

Within minutes, the wind caught the sails. As the hull sped through the water, Allie remained sitting near the stern, letting a dreamy sensation drift over her with the sun and wind on her skin.

His hand on the tiller, Riley watched not only her, but also Devin. She looked relaxed, her hair fiery in the sunlight. Touchable. She looked content, her features soft and loving when she looked down at the little boy snuggled in her arms. She looked as if she was holding her whole world in her arms. Riley rarely thought about Devin as another man's child. He was her son, and too often, Riley wished that they'd gotten this far, that he'd given her all she wanted. But he couldn't. He could offer only so much, and he wasn't sure if she would accept it.

"Bird. Bird."

Allie pressed a smiling kiss to Devin's head as he pointed excitedly at a seagull skimming the water in search of food. "Yes, a big bird." Staring at the waves, she propped an elbow on the rail. "I've always loved being out here. It's so far away from everything."

He'd counted on that. If he'd taken her anywhere else, she'd have shaken her head and taken off before he could have his say. "This is kind of nuts."

Allie sent him a quizzical look. *This?* What was "this"?

"This arrangement," he clarified.

Allie felt her heartbeat quicken. Where was he going with this conversation?

"It doesn't have to be like this. You could stay, move in. We could live together again."

That small flutter of hope within her flew away. He wanted to go back to what they'd had before— an easy in-and-out relationship. When Devin squirmed to the side, Allie firmed her grip on him. Fascinated, he leaned over to stare at the water lapping against the sides of the boat. Canvas flapped in the wind, drowning out his gleeful squeals.

Despite mirrored sunglasses, Riley squinted against the sunlight. "Does your silence mean no?"

"I have more than myself to think about." Allie brushed back hair blown forward by the wind. Did she dare take the chance? If they lived together, and Riley was with Devin day in and day out, wouldn't he feel more for his son? And at his tender age, Devin might not get too attached to Riley if she had to walk away. Only she'd be torn apart. "Would you give me time?"

"I waited two years," he said softly. "I can wait a little longer." He saw the flicker of disappointment in her eyes before she'd veiled it with a smile, and he knew that she still wanted those promises, that commitment, marriage—everything he wouldn't give her.

"Thank you for bringing me here." Leaning close, she kissed him and closed her eyes to absorb the sensation of not only his kiss, but also the oneness of three people—father, mother, child. She could almost believe they were a family for those seconds when his lips lovingly moved over hers, when his large hand rested lightly on Devin's small shoulder.

When Riley drew back, she watched his gaze sweep over Devin's face. Why couldn't he see the strength of cheekbones so like his own? New fathers usually thrilled at finding small resemblances with their child. She wasn't certain he'd feel the same. If he saw too much of himself in Devin, would he feel closer or would he retreat in order to prevent more bonding? She wished she could ask, "Why are you suggesting we live together? *Because you love me? Love Devin?*" She wished most of all that he'd said those words to her.

"Dinner's ready," Allie's mother announced the moment the three of them entered the house. "You all must be hungry." Her voice held the same high expectation Allie had heard in it when she'd called earlier and explained that they were going to the lake. "Out there on the water, everyone gets hungry."

Allie snagged her arm. "Mom, don't work so hard. He's staying," she whispered, then raised her voice for Riley's benefit, "since he probably wants to eat *your* beef stroganoff."

"Stroganoff?" In the past, he'd practically drooled over the favorite meal. "I love your stroganoff, Janet."

"She knows," Allie said, amused.

Like a family, the four of them sat around the kitchen table, sharing good food and lighthearted conversation.

Looking content, Riley wrapped noodles around his fork. Adjacent to him, Janet beamed at having someone to appreciate her cooking talents.

As usual, Devin entertained. "Ice ceam?" he

asked about the dish of whipped butter in the middle of the table.

"No, that's not ice cream. You get ice cream later," Allie promised.

"I know," he replied.

She laughed at his latest favorite expression. "He says that to everything now."

Janet handed Riley a basket filled with hot rolls.

He held up a hand. "No, I can't eat anymore."

"No-no," Devin mimicked, shaking his head.

Riley laughed. "No-no?"

"No-no," Devin repeated, giggling because he had everyone's attention.

"He'll do that all night if you encourage him," Allie said. How much Riley had missed. How much he didn't know about his own son.

"Ice ceam," Devin yelled jubilantly.

Allie bent forward and kissed his nose. "Yes, it's time for ice cream."

For some reason, dessert was always the messiest part of any meal. As Devin's spoon scraped the bottom of the bowl, Allie lifted him from his high chair. "A bath is needed."

"I think he even has it in his hair," Janet said with a chuckle when Allie left the room with Devin. "Would you like more coffee, Riley?"

"I couldn't put anything else in me."

"Do you remember Justin Spencer? He was my neighbor's son and thought he'd be the next Tom Cruise."

Riley smiled with her, recalling the kid standing

on the front porch, bellowing out Shakespearean lines. "What happened to him?"

"He got married. He never went to Hollywood, but he is acting in the community theater." She wrinkled her nose. "He's not very good."

Riley chuckled, enjoying himself while she went on helping him play catch-up about more people he knew.

"Yes, that was Renee Markham," Janet answered in response to his question about a small blonde Allie had known since high school. "She married a musician. I think he's a cellist. Anyway, they have an adorable little girl."

It was clear to Riley that everyone Allie knew had gotten married.

"Allie said that Devin loved the concert you took him to." Janet finished wiping off the counter. "I'm not surprised. I've even seen him bounce to the chug-chug sound of his toy train. Right now, he's teetering between his love of music and baseball. I think it all makes perfect sense. Some genetic traits are inherited," she continued brightly. "Allie loves to sing and plays piano wonderfully. And he's bound to be athletic because—"

"His father was," Allie finished for her, hovering at the kitchen doorway.

Just as quick on her feet, her mother agreed, "Yes, that's true." Concern clouded her eyes with the realization that she'd almost said too much. As if looking for a hasty escape, she started for the doorway. "Devin's in the living room?"

Allie heard the nervous edge to her voice and

hoped Riley didn't. "All bathed. Even his hair was sticky."

Her mother offered a slim, strained smile. "Now that you have company, Riley, I'll leave. I need to make a few calls. Doctors must have to pass a test to prove illegible handwriting to get their licenses. One's chicken scratch is absolutely unreadable." She rambled on, a sure indicator of her uneasiness.

"You're still doing medical transcriptions?" Riley interrupted.

"The business is thriving."

Riley couldn't pinpoint at what moment Janet's mood had changed, but she looked torn, as if she wanted to stay, yet was eager to flee. Did she think she shouldn't have mentioned Devin's father to him? "Thank you for dinner."

"You're welcome," she said, with a glance from one to the other before she scurried from the room.

"You should tell her that Mitch isn't a taboo subject. She looked like she wanted to slink off somewhere," he said, a trace of humor in his voice.

Allie returned a slim smile.

"I know she takes care of your boy here." What was behind the worry suddenly clouding her eyes, too? "What about when you were in Seattle?"

"My aunt was understanding, letting me bring Devin to her store. When he was younger, it was easier. A playard kept him safe and toys occupied his time. But since he started walking, he's grown more inquisitive."

Leaning back in his chair, Riley watched her move to the coffeepot. Slender, she looked as if a good wind might sweep her away, but looks were deceiving. In the past, he'd witnessed her determination, her strong will. Still he had to ask, "It's tough being a single mother, isn't it?"

"Sometimes." Allie poured herself coffee.

Though widowhood wasn't controllable, she'd admitted that her marriage had been failing. He puzzled over a lot of what she'd told him, especially how quickly she'd married after leaving him. By nature, she was a practical, cautious woman. Jumping into anything was uncharacteristic for her. "When you met Mitch, why was he in Seattle?"

"Actually, I met him in Chicago first." She paused as she moved to the kitchen doorway to see where Devin was heading. When he settled on the living room floor with a book, she added, "My mother wasn't feeling well, so I came home to be with her."

"Anything serious?" he asked with genuine concern.

"For her, yes. She fell and sprained her ankle." Allie rummaged in a drawer for a teaspoon. No more lies. After she put Devin to bed, she'd tell Riley all that he needed to know. Even his suggestion that they live together couldn't be taken seriously until then.

"You're off somewhere else," he said about her sudden silence.

Allie gave a shake of her head. "I'm sorry."

"So your mother was stuck on crutches for a while?"

"Yes. You can imagine that."

Riley grinned knowingly. Janet was on the move all the time.

Absently Allie stirred her coffee. How long ago that seemed. "So anyway, I went to Cherished Treasures because it was having a June sale last year, and I'd hoped to find a Blue Willow teapot to add to her collection and lift her spirits. That's when I met Mitch," she said, pivoting away in response to Devin's wail for her from the other room. "I'll be back in a moment..." Her voice trailed off.

In June last year.

Her own words screamed at her. Here she was worrying that her mother had said too much. She was the one who'd slipped up! Maybe, just maybe he hadn't caught the telltale words. Fool! she berated herself. He was a cop trained to observe, to listen for slipups. Still hoping differently, she swiveled slowly to look back at him.

He looked stunned.

"I have to..." She took a step, gesturing with her hand toward the adjacent room. "I have to get Devin," she managed to say. *I have to get away.*

Riley stared after her. He'd misunderstood. It was a mistake. If she'd met Mitch in June last year, that meant Devin had been somewhere between four and six months old when she met her late husband. No older.

That meant... His mind rushed to deny it. He had no baby. She couldn't have been pregnant. With his hands and mouth on her so often, he'd have noticed some change in her body. She wouldn't have left him, knowing she was carrying his baby. *His baby.*

"Riley?"

He looked up, his chest tightening. Had he been blind before this? Denial was suddenly impossible as she stood before him holding Devin, already dressed in pajamas. At first glance, Devin looked like Allie—the same fair coloring, the reddish hue to his hair, the deep brown eyes. But now Riley scrutinized the pudgy face. The bone structure, the high cheekbones, the square shape of his jaw and the narrow bridge of the nose assured him that in later years, Devin would resemble him. No mistake, Riley reflected. His timetable about her marriage was off. It hadn't come quickly after she'd left him. The boy was his. "Devin wasn't his son?"

Unprepared for this moment, her heart pounding with uncertainty, Allie tightened her grip on Devin.

How stupid he was, Riley realized. "He's mine?"

"Yes," she whispered. "You're his father."

His father. He heaved a breath. He wanted to hit something. He wanted to yell at her to quit fooling around, to not lie. He wanted those words not to have ever been said. And underneath all that denying, he felt pride welling up inside him. That little boy with his infectious grin and those eyes that seemed to reach into his soul, that little boy was his. "You weren't going to tell me?" he asked now, anger and disbelief mingling within him.

Control. He was always in control, even now when she'd dropped bombshell news on him. "I meant to tell you."

"Then why didn't you?" he asked in a hushed

tone that scared her more than his raised voice would have.

Allie avoided his stare and crossed to the kitchen for Devin's bottle of juice.

"Are you going to answer me?"

"Let me get him settled first," she said, without looking back.

"What's one more minute?" Sarcasm crept into Riley's voice. "You've already taken two years."

Her back straightened. She'd always expected anger. Unless the man was a selfish rat who'd shrug and walk away as if the child was the woman's problem, he'd be furious about not being told sooner.

"You're right. You're not the same," he said, a quiet rage deepening his voice. "The woman I remembered never deceived."

With difficulty, she swallowed angry words in her own defense and brushed past him to set Devin with his bottle in front of the television. She flicked on the set, selected the channel for his favorite cartoon. Courage and calmness eluded her as she returned to the kitchen. She had no excuses, only good intentions. "I tried to tell you."

Coldness paled his eyes. "Did you?"

"Would you really have wanted to know?" she asked in an angry whisper, facing him. For support, she leaned against the stove. "You always told me you didn't want a family. Why would I include you in our lives when you wouldn't want to be there?"

"I deserved to know. I had rights." Fury like he'd known only once before rose within him. He wanted to take a poke at the delicate chin raised at a prideful angle. It was a thought, nothing more. He'd never placed a harsh hand on her, never hurt her.

That wasn't entirely true, he had to admit. He had hurt her in a different way.

"What would you have done? Married me?"

"Dammit, Allie. Dammit." He spoke low, as if dreading to hear his own words. "How could you pretend he was some other man's son?"

Allie felt as if she'd been slapped. She'd never committed that transgression. Before she had a chance to grab another breath, the door slammed behind him. Drained, she sagged against the counter, her bones soft, her legs rubbery. She slapped a hand over her mouth until her stomach settled. Only then did she move to check on Devin.

Needing more, she dropped to the carpet beside him and enveloped him in her arms. Loving by nature, he scrambled onto her lap and rested his head against her breast.

Allie fought tears. Angry or not with her, Riley had learned he had a son and had shown no hint of joy, not even a trace of pleasure. "My baby," Allie murmured, pressing her lips to Devin's cheek and rocking him. "How can he not love you?"

Chapter Ten

It was impossible to sleep. Restless, Allie awoke hours before dawn. She expected Riley to be more unreachable now. That was a given. What she didn't know was what really bothered her.

Did he hate her? What was he feeling about her? Would he even come back? With too much time to think, she found a bucket and a mop. When upset, she became a cleanliness fanatic. Scrubbing floors worked wonders at calming nervous energy.

After Devin awoke, she hummed every song he liked in order to block her thoughts about last night, about the look on Riley's face. Being entertained put Devin in a giggling mood. In the past, he'd never failed to make her smile with his antics, but this morning she struggled to find humor.

Achingly, she wished for what she'd promised herself she would never look for: Riley's happiness about the news. Blame a too-romantic nature. It made her yearn for one of those theatrical, happily ever after endings where a joyous man crushed the woman against him after learning he was a father.

"Dumb," she muttered.

"Dum," Devin parroted, like he did about most new words lately. In the middle of the living room, he lay on his belly, his eyes glued to the television and his favorite movie about a chimpanzee.

From the other room, her mother sent Allie a worried look. Janet hadn't asked. With a mother's instincts, she'd sensed during a silent morning cup of coffee that the world had tumbled down around her daughter. "Did I...?"

"Mom, you didn't do anything wrong." *Don't worry about us.* Allie truly believed she and Devin could do fine by themselves. She squatted before him. "Want to go in the pool?"

"Poo," Devin replied gleefully, while she started pulling his shirt off.

After she finished smearing sunscreen on him, she kissed his cheek and tightened the tie on his swimming trunks. Only he mattered, she reminded herself.

That was the same thought she'd repeated like a mantra to survive the time alone before. As she had then, she would manage. As then, she would deal with the heartache that made her want to curl up in a corner somewhere.

The touch of Devin's small hand slipping around hers made her want to cry all over again. She resisted. Though young, he caught her moods too easily. "Come on."

"Outide?"

"Yes, outside." On the way to the door, she snatched a towel from the linen closet, then paused and popped her head into her mother's office. "Devin's going swimming."

Ushering him outside to his wading pool, she believed that if Riley had really cared not about her, but about his son, he wouldn't have left. Why didn't he realize that this wasn't about him or her? It was about Devin.

Too many questions demanded answers, but Riley hadn't been ready to ask them last night. He'd gone home, poured a tall drink and wallowed in anger—anger at her for not telling him and anger at himself.

In the morning, he could think more clearly. Before his seventeenth birthday, he'd made a promise. He'd failed before, had vowed he wouldn't screw up someone's life again. Fatherhood wasn't for the reluctant, for someone who fled responsibility, for someone who practiced solitude.

What did he know about being a father? For the past eighteen years, he'd avoided contact with kids. Even back then, he'd been dealing with a seven- and an eleven-year-old. Devin was a baby. Riley knew zilch about babies.

That didn't mean he didn't know about kids. He'd seen enough of them older than Devin caught in an undercurrent of low self-esteem, misdirection and lack of respect for authority. Most of those kids had lacked fathers. More often than he could count, Riley had railed about deadbeat dads. He sure as hell couldn't be one.

Son. He was still reeling from what that one word meant. He remembered his own father, a big man with a deep voice and skin leathered from too many years of working on the ranch in the sun. He'd been stern, tough-minded but gentle with his kids. How did a man learn to gentle his hardness, hug someone as small as Devin and not hurt him? How did he know when to be firm, when to laugh? His father had been a natural; Riley wasn't.

Weary from too little sleep and too much thinking last night, he ran a hand over tired eyes before making a few final notations on a month-old homicide report. Yesterday he and Nick had chased down a good lead and nabbed the perp. Case closed. A welcome-back present to his partner.

Earlier, over a cup of the morning sludge the vending machine produced as coffee, Riley had filled Nick in on his status of instant fatherhood.

Frowning, Nick had given him the silent Vincetti stare for a long moment after Riley's announcement. "That's why she left?"

So involved in thoughts about himself, Riley had forgotten her and the boy. "I guess so."

"Knowing how you feel about marriage and family, I'd guess she didn't want to trap you," Nick said.

Too much truth haunted a man. Deep down, Riley still wanted to lay all the blame in her lap, make it easier on himself. She'd always known where he was, and at any time during the past weeks, she could have told him the truth.

"I'd view her choices as hard ones." With the candor Nick had always revealed, he added, "You sure never hid the fact that you liked your life free of lasting attachments." Shrugging, he said no more.

Nothing was left to be said, Riley realized now, dropping the pen on the desk. Hell, how could he fault her? Hadn't he forced her to shun honesty about their son? He'd told her often enough he never wanted marriage or kids. So he had to accept one fact. He'd let her down when she'd needed him most. So what's new? he mused. He'd done that before to others.

Swearing, he snatched up his car keys, then went out the door. While waiting at a red light minutes later, he thought about their last month together back then. He hadn't been careful. She'd been on an antibiotic for bronchitis. She'd told him that her birth-control pills might fail because of the medicine. Whether or not he wanted to be accountable for the pregnancy, he was.

What a mess.

He already knew he was lousy father material. When he'd tried to carry the responsibilities of one before, he'd failed. He didn't want to be responsible for anyone ever again. He didn't want them in his life. Mostly they shouldn't want him.

So what the hell should he do now?

Minutes later, he stood on Janet's front porch and pushed the doorbell. Why? he wondered. Why would fate do this to Devin, to someone so sweet and innocent? There were other men more deserving. Why hadn't Devin gotten one of them instead of him?

Despite her naturally friendly and outgoing nature, Janet looked wary when he entered her house.

"Is she home?"

"Riley." She paused as if she wanted to intervene, offer some explanation, excuse. "Allie is outside with Devin," she said instead and opened the door wider. "Why don't you join them in the backyard?"

He couldn't flash a grin and alleviate the concern he saw in her eyes, but in passing, he touched her shoulder reassuringly. It was the best he could manage.

"Do you want some coffee?" she asked from behind him.

"Nothing, thanks." He stopped at the kitchen screen door. An idyllic scene, the kind photographers yearned to capture on film, existed before him.

In the shade of a huge willow, Allie knelt beside a small, blue-rimmed pool, her face cast in shadow, her head bent. She smiled—a strained smile—while she poured water from a child's sprinkling can over Devin's legs.

His squeals spanned the distance to Riley. Had Allie held back because she hadn't wanted him in Devin's life?

A sense of being watched made Allie look up. She doubted she could prepare herself for this moment. She expected his bitterness, his resentment, the accusations. Despite a slow-building, cowardly urge to run, when he came near and settled on the grass near

Devin's pool, she joined him. "I didn't know if you'd come back," she said, breaking the silence.

"I want an explanation." He braced his back against a brick border that protected her mother's flower garden and draped his arms over his knees. "Did you leave knowing you were pregnant?"

Her throat felt dry. "Yes, I knew."

Pain darkened his eyes. He remained silent, his gaze riveted to Devin. "Tell me something, anything. Help me understand why you did this."

Because you didn't want love. "After your sister's phone call, you were so quiet, too quiet."

Had she said something then—a word, a hint— and, troubled, he hadn't heard it? He'd been caught up in a world of guilt about his sister.

"You pulled away from me."

What he'd had to face in Texas had made him fold in emotionally. He hadn't wanted Allie with him, hadn't wanted her to see him fall apart. Later, he'd been glad he'd made that decision. He'd wept in his car after seeing his sister. Then he'd gotten drunk. No one had needed to see that. "So you were angry at me?"

"Oh." Allie squeezed her eyes shut. Did he really think this was about hurt feelings, about punishment? "No, I felt sad for you—and for me." She touched her flat stomach, recalling how often during the months when it had blossomed that she'd been tempted to call him. "Mostly I felt sad for the baby I was carrying. I knew you didn't want it."

For the rest of his life, no matter what happened between them, what relationship he nurtured with

Devin, he'd have to live with those words. "Did you think I'd ask you to give it up?"

Her eyes drifted to Devin. "I'd have done that for no one," she said, with the same strength of conviction he'd heard countless times in movies as someone declared he'd die before succumbing to villainous pressure.

"Tell me about Mitch, about your life with him," Riley said.

Allie slanted a look at him. How civilized they were being, speaking in quiet, almost whispery tones. Why? Because they both wanted to scream at each other, whip out accusations of blame?

"Did you know him long before you married him?"

"A couple of months." In a small show of nerves, she fingered the denim of her shorts.

"You weren't married long?"

"Four months."

He did a quick calculation. "And widowed— what? Six months?"

"About that. He died in a small-plane crash. He was flying with a friend to Las Vegas."

Riley pulled a blade of grass from the ground and watched Devin climb out of the pool and toddle toward the hose. Holding it up, he tilted his head to drink from it. "I accused you of passing my son off as another man's. I realize now that you couldn't have done that."

"I told Mitch about you. He didn't seem to care. He asked me to marry him anyway. At first, I refused. How could I marry him when I didn't love him? But he knew I was struggling financially.''

Riley's gut twisted. That struggle was his fault, too.

"He said he loved me. He wanted to give Devin and me what I couldn't give my son.''

Riley's eyes snapped at her. *Our son,* he thought angrily.

"I shouldn't have said yes. My mother offered to help me, but she'd done enough when she raised me on her own. I couldn't do that to her. And there was Mitch offering the easy way.''

Allie swallowed hard. "It was a mistake. What he wanted...well, he wanted me. Married to him, he knew I'd be with him. I would feel I had to. That was something I couldn't bring myself to do with any man after I left you.'' How could she? There was Riley, always Riley and the memories of him.

"In the beginning, we attempted to be the happy family, but it's impossible to forget your wife wants another man when that man's child is constantly near as a reminder.''

She let silence slip over them for a few moments. "He grew despondent.''

Riley made a guess. "Because of your relationship?''

"I thought so at first, then realized the gambling losses were what was really bothering him.''

Riley shifted his shoulders. Two years of her life hadn't been easy for her, because of him. "I guess the big question is what about now?'' It was time to make right more than one wrong he'd caused her.

For the first time since she'd begun talking, he looked at her. "What do you feel now?"

She didn't allow herself to believe in some extra meaning in his question. "I can take care of myself."

"It's not just you now. There's someone else."

"Do you think I need that reminder?" she demanded, temper flaring. Tension from his quiet calmness unnerved her. "I don't expect anything from you. I can take care of Devin and myself," she said heatedly. "I've been doing that for almost two years. I don't need to lean on you. And you don't have to do anything."

"Think again." A steely firmness threaded his voice.

Allie stiffened with uncertainty. What did that mean? Would he challenge her for custody? Why would he? She fought to keep her voice steady. "Have your feelings changed? Do you feel any differently about children?"

She'd always leveled hard questions at him. This one ranked as the hardest. At the dull throbbing in his head, he raised a hand to his forehead and massaged it with his fingertips. "I don't know."

"You'd want one now?"

He raised his head slowly. "That question doesn't matter. I have one."

"No," she said, leaning on anger instead of the hurt for Devin flowing inside her. How could anyone not want him? "No, you don't. I told you. You owe him nothing."

"Maybe you don't understand." Fire snapped in his eyes. "You don't make decisions alone about him anymore. I'm a part of him. Whatever happens, we do this together."

"Why?" She pushed herself to her feet. "You didn't want him before."

He stood, facing her squarely. "I know what I said." Frustrated by his own indecisiveness, he swore under his breath. "But we weren't talking about a person then. He's here. He exists. He's my son." Riley had always kept people at a distance, but he couldn't do that with Devin. "I'm responsible."

Allie felt the knot in her throat and pulled away. He would misinterpret tears, and she couldn't explain them. Too many emotions—sadness, uncertainty, even relief that he knew and accepted everything—wove together. "I always wanted him." Her back to him, she spoke softly as she watched Devin splash in the pool. "He's wonderful, Riley. I'm blessed."

So was his son—he had her. Riley moved closer, stepping into her line of vision.

Words she needed to say threatened to stick in her throat. She made herself speak. "I'm sorry. I'm sorry I kept him from you." It was what she'd wanted to say yesterday.

As if warding off something that promised to harm him, he raised a hand. "Don't. It's my fault, not yours. I gave you no choice." Other men might feel betrayal, hate and anger, but when Nick's words had finally penetrated his thick skull, Riley had known he was the one who deserved the blame.

"You don't hate me?"

"God, Allie, no." Sadness clouded his eyes. "I

could never hate you. Never,'' he said, drawing her to him.

Tears smarted her eyes, burned the back of them. "I don't want anger between us. Devin—"

"No anger," Riley said softly. Lightly he touched her cheek. Whether or not he wanted the responsibility of a child, he had it. "I guess if you'll give me a chance, I'll try to make it up to you."

"You didn't know," she said with a calm that took effort. "How could you be at fault?"

"I cared about you. I should have—"

"What? Guessed that I was pregnant?"

"Why are you making this so easy for me?"

Because her love for him was all she was certain of. But she had no idea what to expect now. Would he leave? Would he suggest that later she come to his apartment, but not mention Devin? Would he sit with his son and try to connect with him?

"Look, I don't have answers. I just can't walk away." He wished he could. Logic told him that they'd done fine so far without him. And they'd definitely do better if he kept out of their lives. But good for them or not, here he was. He knew her pride and felt as if he were walking a ledge close to quicksand. "We need to talk about money, Allie." This wasn't any easier than the rest of what he'd said. "What I'm saying is that you'll never have to go to court for child support."

I don't want any money. Just love him. "I don't need it."

He'd expected this reaction. She never leaned on anyone. He'd battled a similar stubbornness while caring for her when she'd broken her arm. "Well, you'll get it. I'll see a lawyer, make arrangements for you and the boy."

Did he really think that child support was all that Devin needed?

"Allie, I need to do this."

She heard the appeal in his voice.

He could sense her resistance. Why didn't she understand what he was feeling? Because of him, she'd had a difficult two years. He never wanted her to go through another time like that, never wanted Devin to. "And I guess the other big question is do you still want to be with me?"

How could he believe that had changed for her? "I knew before and wanted to be with you. Shouldn't you ask yourself that question instead?"

He had no choice. What he felt for her wouldn't switch off. And he'd prided himself on being a man with scruples. To not be around for his son had never entered his mind, but he wished, yeah, he did almost wish they wouldn't want him. "Answer me," he said softly, touching her shoulders.

Too many unfulfilled dreams of a life with him teased her mind. After he'd learned the truth, she'd expected him to offer financial help, nothing more. That he still wanted to be with her flooded her with a rush of what-ifs, especially one. What if they could have a future together? "You know I do."

He held her tighter. He was a father now. For almost sixteen months he'd been one. Face the truth, he railed at himself. You haven't any idea how to be a father. But for Devin's sake, he had to try his damnedest.

Chapter Eleven

Three days passed. During that time, Allie had finished with another of the mysterious unopened crates
in the storeroom. Already she'd priced several pieces.
Most of them she viewed as foolish investments. Had
Mitch really purchased them to subtly thumb his nose
at his brother and bring one of the family stores to
ruin? Who knew? She could only speculate what his
thoughts had been, just as she second-guessed Riley's.

In fairness to him, she reminded herself that she'd
had nine months to prepare for a child. During the
past seventy-two hours, Riley had been giving his
best effort at being a part of their lives, yet Allie
wondered how often he'd wanted to flee, to turn his
back on them. If she thought he didn't care, she'd
have taken Devin and run from him, but since he'd

told her about his brother and sister, Allie sensed that his reluctance to accept her and Devin into his life had stemmed from a past filled with heartache. Still, drifting along without plans had never been her style. Not before, not now.

Lovingly, Allie smoothed a dust rag over the mahogany bureau. At any time, Riley could unclutter his life. That was the crux of his existence. Get close, but not too close. Stay, but not for too long. Give, but not too much. He wanted them to live together. That was all.

Cradling a morning cup of coffee, she ushered Devin into the storeroom. Because her mother had a deadline on a medical transcription for a neurologist, Allie had brought him with her today.

Earlier a shopping bag full of toys had kept him busy. The store wasn't childproof, so she'd brought his playard along. In it now, he made motor sounds and pushed a toy truck around for a few minutes, then whined his displeasure at being confined.

While Carol completed arranging items for the sale, Allie opened another crate. She unwrapped a candy dish, an oval bowl with a domed cover that bore a tracery pattern resembling a cobweb. But within minutes, she gave up the idea of getting the crate completely unpacked. Arms outstretched and eager to get out of the playard Devin repeatedly called for her. Allie tried to distract him, but he lacked interest in stacking plastic colored rings. Not even his favorite books pacified him.

Aware that someone had entered the shop, she lifted Devin into her arms and wandered toward the main part of the store. A glance at her watch assured her that it was too early for a customer. "Carol, who…?"

Her assistant sent her a grin, then gestured toward the counter.

Riley was holding a glass bride's basket with a wavy, flaring rim. Its stand was an ornate, silver-plated naked figure with arms up as if to hold the base of the bowl. "How much is this?" At her answer, he whistled. "That's outrageous."

"So is the price of most antiques." She shifted Devin to her other arm. "What are you doing here? I thought you'd be at the precinct."

"I had vacation time coming." He sniffed exaggeratingly. "Is that coffee I smell?"

"You are not subtle."

He grinned, picking up the paint can he'd brought in with him.

"Come on. If you want a cup of coffee."

He let her lead the way to the kitchen, then paused to close the door.

With Devin cradled against her hip, Allie swung a look over her shoulder.

Frowning, he was scanning the crates and heavy furniture in the storeroom. "I'll paint, and then help." He had to make up for the time he'd been gone when she'd needed him. He had to in any way that he could. "But you'll pay," he teased, trying to lift the frown from her face.

That they could slide so easily into lighthearted banter relaxed her. "This sounds like a winning deal."

"My thought, too."

In a more serious frame of mind, she contemplated how to use his offer. Her gaze drifted to a bag he'd set on the floor. "What did you bring?"

"I nearly forgot." He leaned to the side and snatched up the bag. It crinkled when he reached into it.

Perhaps emotions were too close to the surface, but everything he was doing seemed to make her want to cry. "What's that?" she asked dumbly as another tiny flutter of hope skittered through her.

"What it looks like, a baseball cap." He stretched toward Devin, who was sitting on the floor, and plopped the child's cap on his head. "Looks good on him."

He looked adorable, Allie thought. "Why did you do this?"

"Why?" Riley gave her a crooked grin. "It's sunny outside."

"No," she insisted, wanting—praying—for words that offered a thread of commitment to his son. "Why did you buy it for him?"

Riley had wondered that, too. For a long moment he stared at Devin.

Beaming, their son took the hat off and put it on again. "Ha."

Aware of Devin's grin and how easily he responded to her moods, Allie smiled in response. "Yes, hat."

"It's not the Hope diamond, Allie. Why make such a big deal about it?" Irritation colored his voice. "If you want, I'll take it back."

"No." She migrated from him, her throat tight. She couldn't be mistaken. Fatherly pride had warmed the blue of his eyes. "Someday you can sit in the bleachers and watch him play."

"Maybe." He never thought so far ahead.

Allie smothered her frustration over his noncommittal answer, one that took away even a hint of commitment. She had to stop being a fool. There had been no hidden meaning in his action.

Riley caught the disappointment in her face before she turned away. He'd hurt her again, but he couldn't pretend with her. He'd wanted Devin to have a cap. He believed in today. After finding himself alone one day, he believed there was no point in planning tomorrows. "So what job do you have for me?"

As Devin scampered to her to be picked up, Allie knew how Riley could really help her. But would he want to? "It would free me if you amused Devin."

Riley felt her watching him closely. He could almost read her mind. Did he want to be with his son? Sensing a test of sorts, he gave her his best grin. "I expected you to need muscle power. This is an easy job," he said, standing and taking Devin from her arms. With no experience, he could only approach his new fatherhood status with a sink-or-swim attitude.

One minute the small warm body was against her, his small arm resting on her upper back. Now Devin clung to his father, his hand snugly curled at the back of Riley's neck. How could he hold him and not feel love? Allie wondered. From the first moment Devin had been in her arms, she'd felt so much of it for him that she'd thought she'd burst with happiness.

"Okay, slugger." Riley scanned the toys strewn across the kitchen floor. "Let's find something to do." He kept the dumb grin on his face until she'd left the room. His eyes met Devin's dark ones, so like Allie's. "Now what? It's just you and me for a while." Could he tell that his father was lost at what to do? "This is going to be a cinch. Right?"

A more questioning look slipped over the boy's face.

"You know I'm new at this." Riley set him on the floor in front of scattered blocks. "So I'll give it my best shot. You give it yours."

In his slow, clumsy way, Devin stood immediately and latched onto Riley's leg, clutching the denim in a death grip. "Up, up."

As Devin stretched up an arm to be lifted, Riley sensed he'd wail if he didn't get his way. Bending over, he gathered him close. A soft cheek pressed against his; little legs wrapped around his waist; the short arms clung to his shoulders, clutching him as if he was special. More than anything, Riley wished that he was.

His child. An intensifying ache swept through him. *Don't rely on me,* he wanted to tell him. *Don't expect too much from me. I'm a man, just a man.*

Several times, between waiting on customers, Allie tried to sneak back and see if father and son were okay, but she was as harried as Carol was at keeping up with customers' questions and purchases. Five more minutes passed, and she still stood behind the counter.

"I always wanted one of these," one customer said with pleasure about the Copenhagen porcelain puppy Allie was wrapping for her. The woman's smile widened as she looked past Allie. "Is he your little boy?"

Allie paused in folding tissue over the woman's purchase, to find Riley close behind her with Devin in his arms.

"I think he needs his diaper changed," he whispered in her ear. "Where's the diaper bag?"

"Oh." She didn't think he was prepared for this duty. "Give me a moment, and I'll change his diaper."

"I'll do it."

Allie knew some diaper changes carried a definite wallop. "Are you sure?"

"Just tell me." He looked up at the elderly woman and grinned. "Morning." He touched Allie's back. "So are there any tricks I need to know?"

She couldn't help smiling. "Take cover, and the tape goes from back to front," she murmured.

His brows knitted. "Take cover?"

"He's a boy."

"Oh, yeah." Riley chuckled, shaking his head as he walked away, but he felt like some ancient warrior marching toward the enemy's camp.

In the kitchen, he set Devin down while he fished in the diaper bag. He didn't really look distressed, Riley decided as Devin banged a wood spoon harder at a pan. And what if it was a nasty diaper?

Bending down, he lifted Devin back in his arms. Then sniffed exaggeratingly. He smelled nothing. "Men stick together." Devin's dark eyes—eyes that sparkled with innocence—were glued to his. "No wiggling, no crying, Devin. And no messes, please."

Allie finished with the customer, then sneaked off to see if help was needed in the other room. The soiled diaper was wrapped neatly and deposited in the garbage can. In typical fashion, Riley had made himself comfortable. With his boots off, he'd propped stockinged feet on an adjacent kitchen chair and was reading a world-events magazine that she'd noticed he'd retrieved from his car earlier.

Standing beside him, one little hand resting on Riley's thigh, Devin teetered on one leg while he tried to slip a foot into one of Riley's boots.

"Need help?" Bending to the side, Riley offered a hand. With a giggle of delight, Devin sunk his whole leg into the boot.

If anything could touch her, it was seeing them, the two males she loved, with their heads close together, their hands touching. It was this gentleness in Riley that had made her fall in love with him the first time around, made her believe there was hope for them, for Devin to have his father in his life.

Without a word, she ambled back to her customers. Throughout the day, several more times, she checked on Devin and Riley. Once, they were playing indoor baseball. Another time the smell of food cooking led her to the kitchen, and she found Riley flipping grilled cheese sandwiches. Certain that Devin was content, and Riley's patience hadn't faltered, she wandered about the store answering customers' questions.

At ten minutes to six, Allie ushered the last customer out and locked the door. Standing behind the counter, she shoved money into a bank envelope for deposit. As she yawned, a masculine arm snaked around her waist.

"You look beat," Riley whispered in her ear.

"Good tired. It was a successful day," she said with a sweeping look around the store. "But I'm ready to go home."

After taking Devin back to her mother's, Riley drove them toward his apartment. "We should start moving your stuff in."

So he hadn't changed his mind. "When?"

"Tomorrow."

"I need to get packing cartons," Allie said, continuing the conversation while they rode the elevator. "We could pick up some tonight."

"Not tonight."

She looked away from him when the elevator doors swooshed open. "We're not doing anything special tonight."

"Sure we are."

Allie followed him to his apartment, catching up while he unlocked the door. "What are we doing?"

Opening the door, he slid an arm around her waist and drew her in with him. "This."

Even before his mouth closed over hers, she'd seen a look in his eyes. No other explanation had been needed.

He didn't bother to turn on lights. Except for flicking the lock, his hands never left her. A sound of pleasure slipped from her throat. Tense days had followed since the last time they'd been together like this. Clinging to him, she closed her eyes and let sensations lull her. She felt a wildness in the mouth plundering hers, in the tongue seeking and dueling with her own, in the hands racing down her body. She felt the coolness of the air conditioner fluttering across her skin.

As if starving for each other, they pushed clothes aside. Her back to the wall, she hooked her legs around his hips. Mouths, opened and hot, met. They came together quickly, their groans mingling with his every thrust until shudders rippled through them, silenced and stilled them.

In the moonlit room, they stood quietly for a long moment afterward, her legs still curled around his, their breaths harsh but steadying, their flesh carrying the musky scent of passion.

Slowly, he moved his mouth down her throat. For so long he'd stifled emotions. Struggled not to let anyone get too close, not even the one person he'd lived each day to see, who'd been a part of his every waking thought. For a little while, he wanted to pretend he could give her back what she offered so generously. "Let's go to bed," he murmured against her skin.

Allie didn't bother to respond. She was already drifting beneath another kiss. Striding into the bedroom, he tumbled with her onto the mattress. There was no patience in him, no gentleness. Hunger driving her, she gripped him to her. She'd give. Keep giving. If he never gave back, she'd live through that, just as she had before. But she'd have this moment and others to cling to, and she would remember what seemed like his desperation to please her. Yes, she'd have this.

Greedily his mouth caught her breast, as his fingers sought the warmth between her thighs. She ran her hands over his back, damp and muscular, and called his name. It was, would always be the only one she longed to say during such a moment. No other, only this man, would ever have her heart.

Reaching down, she curled her fingers around him, heard his moan. With their flesh damp and touching, she could believe in them, pretend that he was hers. His harsh breaths echoing in her ear, he spread her legs and positioned his knees between them.

For an instant, only a second, his eyes met hers before his mouth fastened on hers. Then he entered her. She wanted to believe she saw more than passion, felt more than the heat of his need.

Closing her eyes, she gave without hesitation, her body blending with his, rubbing against him, answering his every thrust. He would accept these moments, her willingness, her body, the consuming heat.

If only he'd accept all she offered—to be there for him always. If only, she mused wistfully, her blood heating. Then all reasoning left her. Breathless, she cried out, melting into him, welcoming more of him inside her.

* * *

Having to move took effort. His heart still racing, Riley made himself shift to ease his weight from her. His arms tight around her, he rolled to his back. He lazily closed his eyes, but felt her movement.

"Do you have any coffee?" she murmured against his throat.

It wasn't a request he'd expected. "You want coffee?"

Raising her face, Allie kissed his chin. "And your bathrobe."

"You'll ruin the mood."

Her hand glided down and over his buttocks. "We're just taking a break, aren't we?"

Smiling, he slid his arm out from under her and moved off the bed. "A short one."

She heard the humor and the promise in his voice. Tangled in the sheets, she watched him tug on jeans. There would never be another for her. While that thought should have saddened her, because deep inside, she knew this joy couldn't last, she felt too content, too close with him right now to care.

"Come on." Standing over her, he reached for her hand. "Or did you expect to get it delivered?"

"I'm up," she said, laughing, and dodged the hand aimed for her backside. "Where's your robe?"

Already headed for the kitchen, he called back, "Behind the bathroom door."

Allie stretched, then padded to the bathroom. Not bothering to flick on the light, she reached for the blue velour robe she'd bought him their first Christmas together. It had been their only Christmas together, one with memories she'd tucked securely in her mind. They'd had only a few ornaments for a tree. At midnight on Christmas Eve, they'd bought it, not noticing until they'd brought it home that it listed so far to the right it looked comical.

Happy days then. Now, too. Heady with love, she didn't want to have doubts—not now, not yet. Tying the belt of the robe, she reentered the kitchen and returned the smile he shot at her over his shoulder. Eager for closeness, she crossed the distance to him. How could so much have been wrong before, yet everything feel so right now? she wondered.

"About those cartons you mentioned earlier. I picked up a few large ones yesterday."

"Good." Allie stepped toward him. "There's more stuff at my mom's than I realized." She took the coffee cup he handed her, then lounged against the counter while he poured one for himself. That's when she saw the letter with the Texas postmark in the garbage can. He'd never opened it, never read his sister's words. How could he do that? How could Allie leave it there? Riley still baffled her. He'd gone to Texas to see his sister. It had been important to him to be there, yet he wanted nothing to do with her now. Why?

Allie's silence made Riley look over his shoulder. "How much more?" he asked, referring to her previous comment.

"A lot."

Because she sounded distracted, he gave her his full attention. All he needed to do was trace her stare to the letter on top of a stack of junk mail in the garbage and he knew where her mind had wandered.

Silently he swore. He should have buried the damn letter. He knew that look on her face. The letter bothered her, and nothing he said or did was going to take her mind off it. "Did you read the return address?"

Her head snapped up. She hadn't. Why was that important? She'd seen the postmark.

"It's from the federal prison in Texas." He sipped his coffee, letting its heat sting his throat. "My sister's in jail. She was going in when I went to see her two years ago."

"Jail?"

"All those years, she never contacted me until then. Then she took the time to find me, to call. I'm a cop. Do you know what it's like to find your sister in jail? She's still there. Five to ten in a federal prison for mail fraud. That letter," he said, with a fierce slice of his hand in the direction of the envelope, "that's the first time she's contacted me since she went in."

"What are you saying? Because she's in jail, she's not your sister anymore?" Allie asked, unable to stifle her disbelief. "Or because of pride you turned your back on her?"

"There's nothing to say."

Suddenly chilled, she pulled the robe tighter around her. "She might want to—"

He turned from her and poured more coffee into his cup.

Allie hugged herself almost protectively. When she hadn't been expecting it, he'd erected another wall between them. "What is it that you feel I won't understand?"

How wrong she was. He dreaded most her compassion, its ability to weaken him. "She made the first move. I went to see her, to help." Ice coated his voice. "Want to know what she said?" He didn't wait for Allie's response. "'So you came. When I needed you, you weren't around.'"

The raw honesty left her breathless. What pain he'd endured! The sister, the little girl he'd lost in the system, hadn't fared well and had blamed him.

"I don't know her, Allie," he said, facing her. "And she doesn't know me. Whatever the reason for her call or her letter, I don't give a damn."

Allie's heart twisted. Oh, but he did. He was being torn apart inside. Everything that made him who he was seemed clearer to her now. She felt the pain of a young boy, the guilt of a man. "I wish you had shared that with me," she said softly.

Sharing came with a price. Too much had gone wrong for him to believe in what most people did—love, marriage, a family of his own. "What would you have done for me? Nothing. You couldn't have done anything."

Allie refused to let the wedge slip between them. She knew of no way to help him, so she followed her own instincts and spoke honestly. "Except hold you," she said, sliding her arms around his waist.

His own vulnerability consumed him.

"Thank you," she whispered, touching his cheek. If he let her, she'd offer comfort he didn't deserve.

"Allie, don't make more of this than what it was. I told you what happened. That's all."

Hurt again teetered near. She resisted it. No words would ease his mood. Smoothing her hands over the planes of his chest, she raised her face and pressed a kiss to his firm, unyielding mouth. *You're mine. You could always be mine, if you'd let it happen.*

He stiffened, willing himself to step away. He couldn't. As before, this slip of a woman held him effortlessly. With her slender arms tight around him and her mouth, so gentle and giving on his, a warm feeling of contentment and a peace he had no right to feel moved through him. With an oath, he scooped her up into his arms, hoping he would never hurt her too much.

Chapter Twelve

"You still own enough shoes to open a shoe store," Riley grumbled. He heard Allie's soft laugh. With the morning sun full on her face, she looked like a teenager sitting cross-legged on the carpet in the middle of her bedroom. As if the night before had never happened, they hadn't said another word about the letter or his sister. That suited him.

Amused by his comment, Allie ignored him and kept packing her shoes in a carton. "There's more in Seattle in storage." Seeing his scowl at the toys that weren't packed yet, like Devin's ball pit and riding fire engine, she thought she'd better prepare him. "I never moved all of my things."

"All?" Seated on the edge of the bed, Riley dragged the shoe carton toward him for taping.

Though organized, Allie had never been quick to throw away anything. "How much more?"

Her eyes danced with a smile. "Lots more." She pushed on the top of a bulging carton to close it. "I've decided to fly to Seattle to make arrangements to have it shipped here."

He shot a look at her. "When are you going?"

"I made a plane reservation for later this afternoon. I thought we should have all of this moved by then."

An obvious question needed answering. "What about Devin? Are you taking him with you to Seattle?"

That he asked meant they were making progress, Allie believed. "Well, it seemed logical to ask my mom to watch him, since she usually does when I'm working." She wondered if Riley's feelings would be hurt that she hadn't asked him. When he nodded agreeably, she squelched the disappointment churning within her. She shouldn't expect so much from him, she knew, but she wished he felt a fatherly desire to be with his son.

Riley squatted beside another carton to tape it. What she'd said was logical to him, too. The biggest concern he'd had for those seconds between his question and her answer was that she would ask him to watch Devin. Being a father came with certain... Finish the thought, Riley berated himself. Being a father came with certain responsibilities. He knew he should want to take over some of the duties with Devin. Most fathers did. He just wasn't ready yet.

Allie ran a hand over the back of her neck to rub

away tension of her own making. She always had too many expectations. She couldn't push Riley into being a father. No one would win then. She had to learn to be patient. Because he'd hidden his emotions for so long, because he'd dodged forming attachments with others, he needed time to get comfortable with having Devin around.

As she went to the closet and stretched toward a shelf for a box, he moved beside her. "Let me." It was heavier than he'd expected. "What's packed in here? A bowling ball?" The humor dancing in her eyes made him smile. "Where do you want this?" he asked, holding the box.

A grin curving her lips, Allie pointed to the floor. "Anywhere. I really don't remember what's in it," she admitted. "High school mementos, maybe." The box did weigh a ton, she decided while reaching for a knife on the dresser to slit the tape stretched across the top of the carton.

"Taking a trip back to your adolescence?" Riley asked as she squatted beside the carton.

"I'd rather not," she said, lifting her high school yearbook from the carton.

Curious, he dropped to his haunches beside her. "Let me see."

"I'll warn you now." Allie let him slip the yearbook from her hand. "I bloomed late."

With his other hand, he caressed her hair. "Well worth the wait."

"You are smooth tongued," she said with a laugh, then dug in the carton again. The weighty object she lifted from a nest of newspapers was a dreadful-looking vase she'd made in a ceramics class.

"You made that?"

She feigned a frown. "Do you have a problem with my—?"

"Masterpiece?" he finished for her.

Allie giggled. "Oh, it is awful." She ran her fingertips over the heavy blue-and-green paint. "It's from my freshman year. I was going through this I-want-to-be-an-artist phase."

"Obviously making that wised you up."

"Ah." She smiled brightly and held up a five-inch-high trophy. "My bowling trophy. Impressed?"

Smiling with her, he leaned close to brush his lips across her cheek. "Always."

"I think it's time to give it a burial," Allie replied lightly, reaching back in the carton. Beneath a few certificates for good citizenship and attendance, her fingers closed over a framed photograph. It was a candid shot of her and Riley standing on the deck of his boat, him in cut-off denims, her in white shorts and a bikini top. The photograph of them laughing, with eyes only for each other, emphasized the wonderful days they'd shared during that Indian summer. She remembered how bright the sun had been, how warm the air.

A soft, reminiscent look swept over her face. Curious, Riley peered over her shoulder.

"We had some good times," Allie said, smiling up at him.

And they would have more. He wanted to give them to her. He'd do anything to erase the bad memories she had because he'd held her so far away from him that she'd felt she couldn't share the most important news in her life. "I remember." He nibbled at her top lip. "Every minute."

It was a concession of sorts, Allie knew. In his way, he was telling her she'd always been a part of him even when they'd been separated.

"Is your mother home?"

Allie released a throaty laugh and angled a look back at him, then pressed her mouth harder to his. "No."

"And Devin's napping?"

She felt the mood between them shifting. "Yes, he's asleep."

The softness in her voice whispered over him like a caress. "Want some more great times?"

Huskily she laughed, turned and fell into his arms, tumbling back to the floor with him.

The moment her plane lifted into the air later that afternoon, Riley felt like a displaced person. An empty feeling clung to him, like some parasite hanging on for survival. Dammit, why couldn't he shrug away the hollow sensation? He was used to being alone. For most of his life, he'd lived a loner's existence.

Allie.

When they were living together, he'd accepted his enjoyment of her, the warmth and passion of their lovemaking, but he'd strived for a separateness he'd known she hadn't felt. He'd felt lousy, aware that, because of him, someone so giving and caring was getting the short end of the stick, but he'd still never yearned for anything lasting.

He could go to the ball field and watch one of the teams from the precinct play baseball, he told himself. Or he could go to a bowling alley near his apartment, a favorite haunt of several detectives. Or he could go to dinner and a movie by himself, like he used to do before Allie had returned to his life.

He didn't want to do any of that. Feeling a need to be with someone else close to her, he went to Janet's. He was barely inside the house when she invited him to dinner.

"I only made macaroni and cheese," she said, a touch apologetically.

Despite a fondness for a good meal with meat and potatoes, Riley would have settled for beans tonight. He needed company, some kind of connection with Allie. He could find that only with Janet and Devin. "Sounds great to me, if you want company."

She tsked at him. "Since when are you company? You've mowed my lawn, washed my car, fixed my plumbing."

"I'd do anything for your food," he said with a wink.

"For that I'll have to whip up something special to go along with the macaroni and cheese." Smiling, she swung back toward the kitchen. "Could you keep an eye on Devin for a few minutes while I finish up in the kitchen?"

Riley noted she didn't wait for his answer. He soon realized watching Devin meant just that.

After bouncing from hitting a golf ball with his toy golf club to shoving a toy truck around, Devin climbed into a toy boat.

"Kezs," he said, dangling keys at Riley.

Riley barely got settled on a chair when Devin took off down the hallway. In a swift move, Riley rose to follow. He'd taken a few steps when Devin reappeared around the hallway corner. Arm outstretched, he held his hand out and curled his fingers toward himself. "Come on, come on," he urged.

"Okay, sport. Where are we going?"

"Come on!" he insisted in that same small voice, repeating his previous gesture.

Riley followed to the guest bedroom, where Allie's scent immediately surrounded him. While they'd been separated, he used to dream of her, see her smile, hear her voice, bring forth that scent from memory. During those years when he'd dreamed of her, she'd been blossoming with his child inside her, had gone through labor and dealt with midnight feedings. She'd been alone, and shouldn't have been. He wondered if he could ever make that time up to her.

"Aa, aa." Devin caught his pant leg and pointed to a wicker trunk.

"Are you sure you're supposed to be in here?" Riley asked, while unlatching the trunk to open it.

Expecting no response, he chuckled when Devin replied, "Yah."

"Yah, huh? Okay." Riley lifted the lid. "Guess you are," he said. The trunk was stuffed with toys.

"Dat." Devin pointed to a xylophone.

Amazing, Riley mused. He was beginning to understand his son's abbreviated English. He reached in and lifted the toy out, expecting Devin to plop on the floor and merrily bang on it. Instead he handed the stick to Riley.

Just about the time he thought he knew what he was doing with Devin, something happened to make him want to call for help. Guessing what his son wanted, Riley joined Devin, on the floor. As if his son had received an invitation, he scrambled onto his lap and leaned back against him.

So small, so vulnerable. What if he let him down? "You scare me," Riley whispered, kissing the top of his son's head as he sat contentedly still.

"If you two can leave your toys, dinner is ready," Janet teased from the doorway.

No one could make a macaroni-and-cheese dinner taste as great as Allie's mother could. Stuffed from too many helpings of it and a huge ham steak, Riley offered to help with the dishes.

"That's what a dishwasher is for," Janet replied. With her eyes she followed Devin move out of the kitchen and toward her piano. On tiptoe, he stretched and fluttered his fingers across the keyboard for a few seconds, then reclaimed his bat. That was discarded quickly, and his interest seesawed from it to the toy golf club, then to giant Legos.

With repeated glances toward the television, where a tape of a dancing dinosaur was playing, he yawned while he grabbed the bat again.

"Nite-nite time," Janet said, lifting him into her arms.

"Ni-ni." He waved a hand at Riley.

Riley knew he could have left it at that. He could have walked out the door, found some buddies and written off the evening as a few hours spent with his son. But he needed more. He felt almost compelled to be more a part of his life. "Do you mind if I stay until he's in bed?"

"Of course not." Janet held Devin out to him. "It's bath time first. I'll run the water if you'll undress him."

That sounded simple enough. It wasn't. Devin squirmed, turning while Riley tried to untie his shoes. Giving up, Riley slid the second one off, still tied.

"Here's his rubber duck." Janet dropped it in the bathtub when he brought a bare Devin into the bathroom.

"You, stay," Riley insisted sternly. "I've never bathed a kid."

An understanding smile warmed her eyes. "I didn't plan to abandon you."

"You'd better not." He gave her an embarrassed shrug before lowering Devin gently into the bath water.

"I'd better tell you—"

Her caution came too late. Devin slapped at the water and splashed it up at Riley.

Getting more than one faceful of water, he laughed. "I get the feeling this is more playtime than serious business."

"How perceptive of you," Janet replied in a humorous tone. "I'll get another towel."

Bath time with a toddler was an experience Riley had never expected. Oblivious as to why he was really there, Devin made a *brrr* sound and pushed a toy boat through the water. Not with any real ease, Riley managed to soap him. Skin soft as velvet was squeaky clean after a final rinse.

"No, no, no, no, no!" Devin yelled, but not about his bath.

Janet stood at the doorway and laughed at her grandson. "I gather his boat is in trouble again."

Amusement rose in Riley. "He scolds his boat often?" She nodded and he shook his head, while Devin repeated the reprimand.

"He does that almost every bath time—puts the boat behind him. But it keeps drifting away, and he gets upset with it." Janet set a towel near Riley. "Here's your towel."

"I doubt it will help." He viewed his drenched T-shirt before wrapping a towel around Devin.

"I should have warned you."

"I had fun." Too much, probably. Little by little, his son was inching his way into his life with the same ease Allie had. Little by little, Riley kept wanting to believe that maybe, just maybe, this time he wouldn't fail the people he cared about.

Wrapped in a towel, Devin kept those dark eyes on him. "Think you'll get used to me?" Riley asked. As little arms wrapped around his neck, he felt his heart melt. "God, no wonder your mommy loves you so much."

"Someone is worn-out," Janet said from behind them a few minutes later.

"Yeah," Riley whispered. Love. Love like he'd felt for Allie filled him. Holding Devin tightly, he'd thought he'd burst with it.

He went home and didn't sleep.

The next night was no better. He spent time with Devin again, and learned in one brief evening that kids his age never sat still, giggled often and fell asleep anywhere when tiredness overcame them. After Devin was in bed, Riley hung around until Allie's nightly phone call.

"You're driving me so crazy I'm forgetting everything else," he admitted to her.

She laughed, sounding pleased. "And what did you forget?"

"How much I could miss you."

"Seriously?"

"I am being serious. I'm losing it early in life. I forgot I have a baseball game tomorrow night, but I'll pick you up at the airport first."

"You don't have to. I'll meet you there. The same baseball field?"

"Same place," he said. "Will you bring Devin?"

She was silent for a long moment. He couldn't blame her if she was surprised. He surprised himself sometimes.

"He'd like being there." She could easily imagine the joy Devin would get sitting in the bleachers and cheering on his daddy. "What time?"

"Seven." With a goodbye, he set down the receiver. He couldn't ignore the need he'd felt just to hear her voice. But he wanted to; he really did.

A gloomy gray sky greeted him at eight the next morning. He crawled out of bed, still feeling like some love-smitten fool. By tomorrow, she'd be living with him like before. No, that wasn't really true. Nothing was the same anymore. Another person, little as he was, dominated their world now. With him, they weren't just a couple; they were a family.

The word twisted his gut. He knew what had happened when he'd had a family before. He'd lost them. He would never forget the heaviness bearing down on him when his parents had died, the inconsolable tears of his brother and sister. He'd tried to do right by them, dammit. But there had been fear in their eyes when the three of them had been alone, sleeping in the car. Riley would never forget the panic on his sister's face, the screech in her voice as she called his name when authorities had taken her from him. He would never forget her angry accusations the last time he'd seen her—in jail.

He was taking a big chance, he realized. He could try to convince himself that he wasn't doomed to failure this time, but what if he was?

Allie returned home at five that afternoon, feeling as if she'd been gone from Devin for weeks instead of a few days.

"Every night you were gone, Riley was here with Devin," her mother said while Allie unpacked her suitcase.

Allie dropped clean panties into a dresser drawer. "I'm glad to hear that."

"I'd thought you'd be more pleased."

She was, and scared to believe that he was beginning to feel an attachment to Devin.

"Allison." Her mother cupped Allie's shoulders and forced her to sit on the edge of the bed. "We need to talk."

"Devin's—"

"He's busy." On the floor, he pounded steadily at plastic pegs with a little plastic hammer. "Do you think I don't understand the reluctance you feel? I had the person I loved turn away from me, too. You're afraid Riley will do that again, aren't you?"

"Everything is going so well, is so wonderful. I know him," Allie said softly. "What if he feels walls closing in on him again?"

"I can't answer if he will or not, Allie, but I've been where you are. I loved your father, but I felt him pulling away."

Like mother, like daughter, Allie mused. They'd both loved men who didn't want a wife and family in their life. Was that similarity the reason why her mother was bringing up the past now? "I wonder if Riley will ever allow himself to make a commitment to us."

"Well, it wasn't exactly like that with your father. We did marry, and he did have to leave often because of his job."

Amazing, Allie mused. Her mom was still defending him. With a mother's instincts, Allie glanced sideways to see Devin ready to open a bedside-table drawer. Before he got into mischief, she settled him down with a crayon and paper. "I never understood how you could be so understanding. I remember him going and sometimes not calling for days. He was so secretive."

"Yes, he was, but you know why. He worked for the government, Allie. Sometimes he couldn't tell us where he was."

As a diversion from her own thoughts, Allie urged her to talk more about him. "Is that an excuse for his not being there when we needed him? Don't tell me that every time he walked away, it didn't hurt you."

"Draw," Devin insisted, looking up at Allie and handing her the crayon. Allie dropped to her knees and bent over his paper to draw a circle and a smiley face. He didn't seem to care what she scrawled alongside his scribbled lines, he simply wanted them to do the drawing together. Leaning close, she kissed the top of his head. *You could teach your father lessons. He's never learned that wanting to be with someone would make his life happier.*

"Yes," her mother finally answered, "it hurt terribly when your father left. But we were better for it. That's why I asked him to go."

"No, he wanted to leave," Allie reminded her, surprised that she still felt such bitterness after all these years at how easily he'd done that. "You simply made it easy for him."

"There was danger in his life. I think he tried to be with us. Maybe he loved us too much."

"Love?" Allie stood and swung a look of incredulity at her. "How can you say that?"

"He never knew where he'd be tomorrow, so how could he tell me?" Janet said with a depth of understanding Allie doubted she herself would ever possess. "It took time," she continued, "before I understood. I was younger then. I had a child. I worried about you, about how hard his absences were on you. Angry, I accused him of not wanting to be a husband, a father."

Vividly Allie recalled the painful scene. "He didn't argue that you were wrong."

"No, he didn't," she said with sadness. "And I believe I know why. He felt he would hurt us more if he didn't let us go."

"Are you saying he was protecting us?"

"Does that seem so strange to you—that he loved us so much he let us go? Sometimes I wonder if that's what Riley believes, too. Isn't it possible that something—something that hurts within him— makes him pull away? I don't know," Janet said with a shake of her head.

Allie felt suddenly sick. *But I do,* she mused. When he'd talked about his brother and sister, she'd sensed his guilt. Did he think he would hurt Devin and her, too? Did he believe anyone who loved him would be hurt?

It was dusk when Allie arrived with Devin at the ball field. Walking up to the bleachers, she assumed from the yelling that the umpire had garnered everyone's attention with an unpopular call.

"What a bum," Joe Morez's wife yelled. "He... Allie!" she practically screeched.

In between plays, Allie visited with old friends she knew from two years ago. Like a sorority, policemen's wives offered easy acceptance to a new member. Not only did they welcome her back, they also introduced her to one uniformed officer's latest girlfriend.

"She's kind of airy," Joe Morez's wife commented about the woman. "But we all liked her immediately."

Allie nodded, narrowing her eyes against the glare of the setting sun to watch Riley at third base, snag a grounder and shoot it to first base for a third out.

"That umpire needs glasses," one of the players grumbled as the men came off the field.

Riley let those words drift by him as he spotted Allie. She looked beautiful bathed in the final glow of sunlight, her hair flaming.

With his approach, she lowered her sunglasses. "Hi."

His eyes never left hers as a pang of desire curled within him. Holding Devin in her arms, she moved forward to meet him halfway. When they stopped, inches from each other, he framed her face in his hands and kissed her hard, twisting his mouth across hers until he heard her soft, barely audible moan, until he knew she was aching as much as he was. "That might hold me," he whispered close to her lips.

Allie heaved a deep breath. Her heart hammered against her chest; her mouth burned as if he'd branded her. He couldn't be so loving and not love her.

"When did you get here?" he asked, ignoring the hoots and whistles of teammates because of their kiss.

"A few minutes ago." She rested a hand against his lean rib cage. Beneath her fingers, she felt each breath he drew.

"How did the packing go in Seattle?"

"Everything is supposed to arrive tomorrow morning. I talked to my mom about going to your place and waiting for the movers." Laughter brightened her eyes. "Expect chaos when you come home."

"Hey, Garrison, you playing or not?" one of the players yelled.

"Not," another gibed.

Riley's hand closed over hers in a gesture more intimate than a seductive caress. "We need to talk."

So serious, Allie mused, before rejoining the others on the bleachers.

While she played catch-up about who'd had a baby, who'd gotten married or divorced, Devin, on her lap, watched the playing on the field and clapped his hands enthusiastically whenever a ball was hit, whether it was foul or not.

"He's so sweet, Allie," Joe Morez's wife said.

"But the terrible twos are approaching," Kate Dolan teased. The mother of two sets of twins, she qualified as an expert on kids.

Stepping into the conversation as he came from the playing field, Bob Dolan said between breaths, "Remember Jimmy?"

"Do I ever," Kate answered with a laugh. "That's the year he started taking everything apart."

"Still does," Bob reminded her. He sent a loving look at their four-year-old, who was chasing another officer's six-year-old daughter. "I warned Riley."

"Warned?" Allie asked, puzzled.

"Told him being a father is a tough job. But worth it."

She remained quiet, caught up in a thought. No one had asked her about Devin's father. So Riley had to have told people that Devin was his son.

"We were thrilled to hear the news," Kate chirped, confirming Allie's thought.

Allie nodded, tightening her arms around Devin as he jiggled on her lap with his excited clapping. If Riley wasn't proud of his new status, would he have told people?

"Skunked them," one of the players said proudly when the game ended and the men wandered from the field to join wives and girlfriends sitting on the bleachers.

Sitting shoulder to shoulder with Allie, Riley watched Devin touching his baseball glove in fascination, and he faced what he'd dodged until now. He didn't want to give them up. He could do better this time; he would do better for them than he'd done for his brother and sister, he promised himself. Tilting back his cap, Riley handed Devin a baseball.

"Baw," Devin said enthusiastically, giving Riley one of those grins that touched his heart.

With all his might, Devin tossed the ball toward the ground, rousing comments.

"Watch out, Garrison, we've found your replacement," one of the players taunted lightly.

Aware of the attention, Devin leaned back and turned his face to Allie's breast with a shyness that emerged whenever too many people surrounded him.

Laughing, Allie glanced at Riley. He was looking at Devin. In his eyes was tenderness, and something more, something she'd never seen before. She decided he looked charmed—she had been since the moment she'd seen Devin crying for his first breath of life. Was Riley beginning to love him, too? Was something unexpected and wonderful happening? With all her heart, she wanted to believe that. Cuddling Devin tightly, she prayed for what only months ago had seemed like an impossibility.

As usual after a game, the men stood around for a bit and replayed the good and bad moments of it. With no activity to distract him, Devin fell asleep. Her arms growing numb from his weight, Allie decided to stroll with the others to the parking lot and wait for Riley in her car. One by one, cars pulled away.

In charge of equipment, he returned to the field to collect the bases. Gently Allie placed Devin in his car seat, then stood beside her vehicle, waiting. The sound of feminine voices shifted her attention from Riley hauling the bat bag over his shoulder to women emerging from a park building and heading to their cars.

Alone in the parking lot, Allie settled behind the steering wheel as the park's lights were switched off.

Darkness surrounding her, she peered at Riley loading equipment into his car. "I'll meet you—"

Her voice was drowned out by a scream. Ear piercing, the cry for help echoed through the empty park.

Allie jumped out of her car. Riley was already running across the field. "Call for help," he yelled back at her.

That was all she could do; shakily dialing 911 on the cell phone in his car, and then an ambulance, because of the woman's scream. Her heart pounding, she waited beside her car and peered through the inky darkness at the park building. She couldn't see anything.

Minutes passed like an eternity before cruisers arrived. Allie pointed, sending uniformed officers racing in the same direction as Riley had. An ambulance wheeled into the parking lot. Ambulance attendants ran toward the officer beckoning to them.

Allie's throat threatened to close with her own fear. In the car with Devin, she hunched forward over the steering wheel. Don't let your imagination go crazy, she railed at herself, but there was nothing worse than waiting when someone you loved was in possible danger. She wanted Devin to know the man who loved sports and laughed easily at himself, the man who his mother loved. It wasn't right for her son to never really know his father.

Allie peered harder as she saw movement. The fear inside her slithered away when Riley emerged from the shadow of some trees. Behind him, two uniformed officers flanked a handcuffed man.

She knew the code cops' wives and girlfriends

lived by: never let him see you emotional when he's doing his job. She drew several deep breaths, then rolled down her window to talk to him. "What happened?" she asked with a calm that amazed her.

"Some guy tried to attack a woman, Clara Venton. She's all right. And we got him, but I'll be here awhile." He reached into his pocket, withdrew his apartment key and handed it to her. "You and Devin go home." He leaned forward and gave her a quick kiss. "I'll be there as soon as I can."

Home. Allie stared after him. Did he realize what he'd said to her?

Chapter Thirteen

Curled on his sofa, Allie waited nearly two hours, watching television. She knew she'd dozed because she'd missed the scene when Whoopi Goldberg announced to Demi Moore that she'd been contacted by Patrick Swayze's ghost.

Sipping coffee, Allie looked up as the door opened. Riley looked tired. "Bet you're hungry." She roused herself from the sofa and met him halfway, pressed her cheek to his.

"You weren't exaggerating about the mess, were you?"

She drew back and viewed his living room with him. It was a disaster, with boxes stacked against walls, Devin's toys everywhere. When she'd come back from the ball field, after putting Devin to bed, she'd shoved cartons around to make a path to the living room. "Told you so," she said lightly. "I'll make you something to eat." She slipped free of the hand touching her waist and took it to draw him into the kitchen with her. "Want an omelette?"

"You don't have to."

Allie nudged him toward a chair. "I want to."

He was starving. And exhausted. He'd gotten little sleep the past few days. Today he'd worked late, then had rushed to the ball field. "Did he ever wake up?" he asked about Devin, who was sleeping in his playpen.

"He didn't stir," Allie said, setting a cup of coffee on the table in front of Riley. While she cracked eggs in a bowl, she caught him surveying the living room again. "I told you to expect a mess. When the sale is done tomorrow, I'll have more time to get everything put away." Because he was so quiet, she wondered if the woman had been injured more than he'd initially indicated. "Is the woman okay?" she asked as she whisked the eggs.

"More scared than hurt." Riley tugged off one baseball cleat, then the other. "She was all right when I left the hospital." Her family had arrived—a husband and a daughter. Crying, they'd embraced her. They'd been there for her when she needed them.

As if he had no choice, his gaze drifted to the letter on a shelf above the stove. He couldn't say why he'd retrieved it from the garbage. After all these years, what could his sister want? When he'd last seen Cindy, she'd screamed at him that she never wanted to see him again. And his brother? Who knew where

Brandon was, what kind of life he'd had, what kind of trouble he'd seen or been in, what pain he'd suffered.

Turning from the refrigerator with cheese and an onion in her hands, Allie saw Riley standing near the shelf, staring down at the envelope in his hand. Quietly she poured the eggs into a frying pan. As he fingered the crumpled letter, she didn't move, fearful that if he remembered she was near, he'd put the letter back.

A second passed. Then another. Gently she folded the egg mixture over the diced vegetables, making sure the spatula didn't scrape the frying pan. And she watched, waiting while he ripped open the envelope.

His shoulders rose and fell as if he was drawing hard, steadying breaths. His stillness frightened her.

Allie flicked off the burner and stepped closer to him to touch his hand.

Eyes filled with unbearable sadness met hers.

"What's wrong?"

"My brother..." He stood straighter, pushing away from the refrigerator as if denying the need for support. "My brother contacted Cindy."

Allie didn't know what to say or how to react. Was he happy? Was he upset, angry? *What do you feel?*

"He contacted one of those agencies that helps you look for missing family members. I guess with nothing else to do in jail, Cindy had done the same thing. He came to see her."

"He's all right?"

"That's what she wrote." He tossed the letter on the counter. All that he'd tried to forget slithered over him. So did a realization: families were for other people, not him.

Allie couldn't stand not knowing. "Why did she write?"

"She wanted me to know his phone number."

Allie sighed with relief. For a moment, she'd feared neither of them wanted him in their lives. She'd thought that was why she'd seen such anguish in his eyes. She stared at the discarded letter. "Aren't you going to call him?"

"No, I'm not." He pivoted toward the stove. "Is the food done?"

If only she could understand what he felt. If only he'd open his soul to her.

Because she didn't move, he reached for the spatula and lifted the omelette onto a plate.

The silence between them pounded in her ears. "Will you please tell me what you feel?"

"Why?" Some of the old anger was back in his voice. "Why do you need to know that?"

"Why?" She felt as if someone had filmed her life and she was walking through a rerun of two years ago. "I love you."

He didn't want to hear those words, didn't want to be tempted to say them back.

"I want you to love me enough to trust me." Again he said nothing. He was only several feet away from her, but she felt him pushing her away. "If you can't, we've gained nothing." Silently, she waited, desperately not wanting to believe that.

He fought himself more than her. From the beginning, he'd known how wrong he was for her, how much he could hurt her, yet he'd been unable to stay away from her. Earlier, he'd even thought about asking her to marry him. "I can't be what you want."

He was closing the door again, and she didn't know how to stop him. "What does that mean?"

He couldn't meet her stare, see the pain he was causing. He took in the toys strewn across the floor, the cartons filled with her possessions, Devin sleeping in his playard. Allie herself, standing in his kitchen. The scene was complete. Like before, two people would rely on him. Long ago, he'd had independence forced on him. Almost half his life he'd freewheeled without anyone to answer to, anyone to worry about or feel responsible for.

Now everything he'd distanced himself from was a breath away. He'd had a family already and had lost them. Why should he have another, mess up again? He took a hard breath against the tightening in his chest. "Allie, you want too much."

A painful realization caused her to jerk. She could love him until the day she died, but he'd never offer what she yearned for. "And you want too little." The end was near, she knew. Nothing she could do or say would alter what was happening. "Every time you get too close to letting yourself care, you back away."

"Be glad I do," he said angrily, knowing he had to make her want to leave. "I never pretended with you." All this time with her, and she didn't realize yet that he didn't have the right stuff for her, for Devin. Riley couldn't take care of others, couldn't be there when they needed him. What Allie wanted from him meant loving people so much he'd have to face all the inadequacies he'd run from for nearly two decades.

"Loving means giving, sharing." She heard her voice crack with emotion and struggled against it. "You don't understand that." He stood stoically before her, his expression unreadable. His silence seemed to say it all. "Be honest. What you're really saying is that you don't want any of this." Emotions hammered at her. "You want to get out of here now, don't you?" she asked, because she wanted, with all her heart, for him to tell her she was wrong.

"You're going to force this, aren't you?"

She supposed she was, she had to, she realized in that moment. For Devin's sake. As he got older, he'd be hurt by his father's inability to love him. A remembrance of her own youthful heartache because of her father made her almost overprotective of her son. She vowed that she'd never let Riley into Devin's life if there was a chance he'd do the same to him.

"Okay," he returned with deliberate coldness. He'd hurt her, but better a little bit now than a lot later. "I never wanted some cozy dream of family and a house with a white picket fence. That's your dream."

Allie dodged the pain vibrating through her. She couldn't give in to it now. Maybe later, but not now. She grabbed her shoulder bag from a nearby chair and moved to the playpen. "I love him," she said softly, lifting Devin into her arms. She was grateful he hardly stirred. "He's the most important person in my life," she whispered. "Unless you can say the same, he doesn't need you. I won't let Devin settle for less than he deserves—someone who'll always be there for him, who'll be there when he awakens in the morning, who'll put him to bed at night. Devin deserves a full-time father."

Riley said nothing, as if waiting for her to make the final move.

"There's no point in talking about this anymore," Allie said tightly.

"Whatever you want, Allie," he said, with as little emotion as he could manage.

You. I want you. I want you to want us, a family. She kept the words silent, reaching the door without looking back. Though her vision was blurry, she stepped into the hall with her son in her arms. She held back a sob. She didn't want to weep, to hurt so much.

Hugging Devin, she rushed to her car. Love. Why was it so hard for Riley to give that to her?

Time crept along. It always seemed to speed by in the good times and drag during miserable ones, Allie reflected. The light of morning filtered through the venetian blinds in her mother's kitchen. Allie still wanted to curl up somewhere and cry. She refused to give in to tears. This heartache was of her own making. She'd expected too much—again. It was her fault she'd fallen in love with the wrong man, the one who wouldn't give love back to her.

As the sun inched above the horizon, she ambled outside and sat on the back-porch swing. She hadn't slept well. Love, she realized, was useless if it was one-sided. As she'd tried to get closer, Riley had again distanced himself. What would happen now was up to him. She knew he wouldn't be entirely out of her life, because of Devin. Would he want to see him regularly? Or would he simply contact his lawyer and arrange for a check to arrive every month?

And what would she do now?

Through the screen door behind her, she heard her mother running water into a kettle to make her morning cup of tea.

Allie labored to her feet, then ambled into the kitchen. To her relief, her mother had already left the room. Allie didn't want to answer questions, explain.

After she fed Devin, she carried him to the other bedroom for a diaper change. She had no time for self-pity. She'd be too busy at the shop.

Attuned to her every mood, he frowned, mirroring her, when she bent over him. His eyes stayed on her while she made herself carry on a silly monologue about his stuffed piggy, his favorite television show about a green-and-purple dinosaur, even his favorite snack—cheese.

"Cheese," he repeated.

Standing him up, she tugged up his denim shorts. "Maybe it's best it's just you and me," she whispered against his ear.

Half an hour later, with no more than a nod to Carol, Allie rushed toward the back of the shop to tackle paperwork before the store opened. A few unpaid bills had been handled, though she had a humdinger of one from a shipping company. Studying it, she realized the bill was for the four crates of junk in the storeroom.

"Allie, do you want me to pack this for Mrs. Kilerman?" Carol asked from the doorway, holding up a large Hummel statue of a little girl sitting on a tree stump. "That's what you told me yesterday."

"Yes, we're to keep it until she returns from her cruise." Yesterdays didn't always matter. Forget what was, Allie told herself for what seemed like the umpteenth time.

Advertising flyers and word of mouth caused an early morning rush in the store. Allie had always prided herself on having a good business mind, and she made sure customers signed their names and addresses to a sheet of paper. If in the future she was ever able to recoup her losses, she'd have customers to send an announcement to.

In the meantime, she could go back to data-processing work until she saved enough money to start up the store again. She'd take a few trips to Wisconsin or Minnesota. Farm auctions inevitably included the sale of family antiques. A year, maybe two, and she might be able to start over.

By late afternoon, much of the inventory was gone. To Allie's amazement, one woman purchased an awful-looking glass vase engraved with cherubs that Allie had uncovered in one of the crates. Another woman whose daughter collected dolls gave her a deposit to hold all of the ones on hand for her. Tomorrow she would return with the rest of the money.

A buyer for the historical society thrilled at the sight of a tapestry of a Louis XV hunting party.

The day was hectic. For that, Allie was grateful. Aware of her situation with Jason, Stefan hand delivered Mrs. Manford's check for the mahogany bureau. Before he left, he announced that he'd be back with her because she'd indicated interest in a wool rag rug.

Toward the end of the day, Allie ran the woman's check and all the money from the sale to the bank, then drove toward Jason's shop.

He greeted her with a triumphant smirk. "So you've come to your senses." He didn't wait for her response. "I'll call my lawyer and have papers drawn up giving me ownership of the property."

Biding her time, Allie wandered the room, which contained several priceless antiques that she thought belonged in museums, not an antique shop. "Why did you want Mitch's store?"

"You're not one of us." His chin lifted to an arrogant level. "It belongs to the family."

Meaning him, Allie knew. While he stared gloatingly at her, she opened her shoulder bag and withdrew a check made out for the full amount of the loan.

His brows bunched as he stared at the check she'd set on his desk. "What's this?" he asked with disbelief. "There wasn't enough value in the store for you to—" He cut his words short. "You're good," he said snidely. "How did you get your latest to give so much money to you? That's what happened, isn't it?"

It was none of his business how she was paying back the loan, how she'd emptied a savings account she'd sacrificed to build.

With his thumb and index finger he lifted the check and turned it over as if inspecting it. "I shouldn't be surprised that he helped you with your bills. I knew he would."

Impatiently, Allie waited for Jason to sign the IOU as paid.

"How old-fashioned of him. Playing the chivalrous knight for the damsel in distress. I thought he was all bluff when he came to me like some great rescuer." Disdain crept into his voice. "I should have known then that you'd twist him around your finger like you did Mitch."

His words sinking in, Allie took a moment to gather her thoughts. She'd known the two men had seen each other at her mother's and again at her shop, but Jason was talking about a third encounter, here in his shop. "When did he come?" she demanded.

"I don't remember." Jason scrawled his signature on the IOU. Suddenly confused, Allie insisted on answers. "Yesterday? A week ago?"

"A couple weeks ago," he said, shrugging in disinterest. "He came in here indignant, telling me you weren't alone." He released a semblance of a laugh, but didn't look amused. "Women like you hook your claws into the first man who comes your way. You're very good at manipulating men."

Allie ignored his final sarcasm, grabbed the IOU and, head high, headed for the door.

Jason's words echoed in her mind while she was

driving. Weeks ago Riley had seen Jason. Before Riley had known Devin was his son. And he'd made sure Jason knew that he'd stand beside her, that he'd be there for her. Why? Why would he do that, then shove her out of his life?

Her mother's words came back to her. What if she was right? Allie knew his guilt. What if Riley's love for her and Devin had made him push them away?

Telephones rang around Riley. A perp in handcuffs shuffled through the precinct hallway, cussing the uniformed officer with him. The dull, throbbing ache in Riley's head intensified. He could work through noise, but thoughts of last night, of the sadness in Allie's voice, the glimmer of tears in her eyes blocked his concentration.

Why the hell was he feeling so lousy? He'd done the right thing. He didn't want to screw up again. Didn't want to hurt the person he loved most. By herself, Allie would do a great job with Devin.

He banged a desk drawer shut, ignoring the stares of other detectives. It didn't matter that he loved her. He couldn't go through all that tugging on his emotions. He couldn't stand to feel the unbearable weight of more guilt when he bungled things up again.

Damn, this was worse than the last time. More than loneliness engulfed him. He felt as if someone had cut out his soul.

"Detective Garrison?"

Unconsciously he clenched his jaw as his annoyance intensified. He raised his head and scowled at the two people in front of his desk. Only a second passed. Though a few bruises lingered on the woman's face from the assailant's attack, Clara Venton looked remarkably well.

"Mrs. Venton." Riley shoved back his chair and stood in response to the hand that the man beside her offered.

"Detective Garrison, we wanted to personally thank you," her husband said.

Riley understood that victims sometimes felt a need for more than the closure of seeing the criminal in handcuffs. "Do you want to sit down?"

"Yes." The man nodded. "If you have the time."

Riley gestured toward the nearby chairs. He had all the time in the world.

"We learned you were off duty that night," Mrs. Venton murmured. A distant look clouded her eyes, as if she was recalling the darkness, the glimmer of a knife blade, the fear when she'd been pressed against the door of her car.

Riley responded with the truth. "Cops are never off duty."

Husband and wife exchanged smiles.

The husband bowed his gray head for a second. "Regardless, you were the one who was there."

"I only did my job. That's all."

"Detective, I can't take lightly what you did. It's because people like you care about others that I didn't get hurt," Mrs. Venton insisted.

Care about others. Riley frowned. He supposed he did care about others. Because of his work, he'd chosen to be accountable, committed to people every day.

"And because of your courage," she added.

Courage. Riley felt a mirthless laugh threatening to slip out. *Can't you see that I don't have any courage? I can't tell a woman who means everything to me that I love her. I can't even make a phone call to a brother I haven't seen in eighteen years.*

The man gripped his wife's hand. "After my wife was taken to the hospital, I called our daughter. She lives here, but she's on her own. She came, frantic. Of course, I assured her that her mother was all right, but before the evening was over our sons had flown home and another daughter who lives in Boston called."

Riley played a good listener, unsure what they were trying to convey.

"I'm rambling on," the man said. "But what I want to tell you is that out of something terrible, we received something wonderful." When Riley looked puzzled, he added, "I should explain. Over the years, our family has drifted apart." He stopped and glanced his wife's way.

She nodded encouragingly.

"It happens," the man said. "We get separated by distance, by time. We've been going about our lives, forgetting each other. Then something happens, something reminds us of what matters most."

Riley shifted in his chair. He knew all about a family being split apart.

As the man stood, Riley drew himself back to his surroundings and rose from his chair.

Mr. Venton pumped Riley's hand. "I don't know what I would have done if I'd lost her." Emotion made his words come out haltingly. He drew a hard breath, as if willing away the rush of feelings revisiting him. "We all want to thank you, but words don't seem sufficient. Sometimes it takes a fright to remind us that family is more important than anything else. That no matter what, we should never forget each other."

His wife smiled. "He knows that, Henry."

Riley shook his hand, watched them leave, then sank to his chair. Never forget them, the man had said. But Riley had; he'd wanted to. After too many losses, he'd emotionally crawled in a hole for one reason—to forget.

A tightness in his chest made him breathe harder as he reached for the telephone receiver. He gripped it fiercely, in the manner of someone afraid to let go.

With his other hand, he fished out his sister's wrinkled letter. He couldn't have said why he'd taken it from the shelf and stuck it in his pocket this morning. He stared at it, kept staring so hard at his brother's number that the image blurred. Make the phone call. Make it, dammit!

A dryness in his mouth made him swallow hard while he punched out the numbers. He'd given up on the idea of family. But he had a woman who loved him. A son. Two people bound to him for life. The pressure in his chest moved up to his throat.

He counted ten rings, then eleven. One more and he'd hang up. The ringing stopped, and a male voice, a stranger's voice, answered.

"Brandon?"

"Yes."

Talk. Say something.

"Who is this?" his brother asked, obviously annoyed by the silence.

"It's Riley."

Chapter Fourteen

Allie never felt the satisfaction she'd expected after handing Jason that check. She was hurting, and hating it. Closeting herself in the storeroom, she began yanking at the metal clips on the last crate.

Keep busy. Think about anything but Riley.

From one crate, she'd unpacked pressed-glass napkin rings. Though they were scarce, they weren't expensive. However, she'd stopped to contact a woman who collected Victorian glass and was eager to buy them. She'd also unwrapped a creamer with a scalloped-rim, bucket-shaped bowl and ribbed feet. Made of pink slag glass, it was valuable and a rare collectible, created during the last century. She placed it and two more pieces—a toothpick holder and a tumbler—in a locked cabinet. Another phone call assured her that a potential buyer would come in before closing.

Allie honestly expected to find nothing else valuable. Most of the glassware had been reproductions. The porcelain pieces, though collectible, were from the last century.

"You saw Jason?"

Allie snapped to her feet and looked back to see her mother standing in the doorway with Devin in her arms.

"Yesterday you said that if the sale went well you'd deliver the check to him. Did you?"

Yesterday seemed like a million hours away now. "Yes, I saw him."

"Tell me," her mother said anxiously. "I couldn't wait until later to find out. What was his reaction?"

Allie strained for a smile. "He was his usual obnoxious self." Resuming her battle with the metal clips, she pried the crowbar under one, not bothering to share Jason's snide remarks.

"Allie?" Janet inclined her head, forcing Allie to look at her. "You don't look happy at all, and I would have expected..." She was silent for a long moment. "Something has happened with Riley, hasn't it?"

Allie avoided her deciphering stare. In a stall tactic, she lifted the lid from a crate that she assumed held more glassware. What was the point in putting off this moment? she wondered, and prepared herself for her mother's usual speech about him being perfect for her. "It's over." Even saying the words knotted her throat.

A mixture of confusion and concern settled on Janet's face while Allie shared some of the most painful moments she could remember.

"But he didn't say that he didn't want to be Devin's daddy?" her mother asked.

Allie wondered if her mom had been born optimistic. "He said he wanted no cozy dream of family." Her eyes smarting, she blinked hard. Tears were useless.

Leaning closer, her mother touched her hand. Allie expected her to plead a case for Riley. Instead, she draped an arm around her shoulder.

"I'm all right," Allie insisted, taking a deep breath.

"Are you?"

"Yes," she said, because of the anxiety she heard in her mother's voice. "I just need to keep busy." She swept a hand toward the crates. "Four of these were delivered right after Mitch and I were married," she said, to detour the topic away from Riley and herself. "I completely forgot about a conversation Mitch and I had about them. He told me he had taken a trip to Austria. These are from the estate of the last member of an old family. When the man died, his possessions, in storage in the cellar of his estate, were sold sight unseen." She knew now that her first impression of Mitch's purchases had been wrong. The odd assortment hadn't been because he'd been trying to play some mind game with his brother. He'd simply been stocking his store, but he'd lacked the knowledge of what was valuable and what wasn't.

"Allison, about Riley—"

"Allie, Mrs. Manford is here for the mahogany bureau," Carol said from the doorway.

Allie yanked off the top of the crate. "Tell Stefan I'll be right there." If it hadn't been for Stefan's earlier visit with Mrs. Manford's check, she would still have that visit to Jason hanging over her head.

Bending over the crate, she frowned at the abundance of packing material lining it. Intending to unwrap it later, Allie merely nudged the excelsia aside to peek at the contents. Her hands stilled, her heart stopped. "Oh, Mitch."

Very elaborate and of the rococo style, the bronze clock's gilt case bore a swath of swirling leaves and a nude lounging at the top.

"Allison?" Concern filled her mother's voice. "What's wrong?"

Her heart was pounding now with the realization of what something so valuable meant for her and Devin's future. "Oh, Mother." Allie couldn't stop the tears. She could almost believe fate had decided to smile on her. Almost. "It's start-up money."

Over Allie's shoulder, Janet peered at the find. "It's *that* valuable?"

Nodding, Allie pointed to the artist's signature.

"Baltazar, Paris," her mother read. Hope brightened her eyes. "Does this mean you can keep the store?"

"Yes, I can." Allie felt an excitement that seemed totally at odds with the sadness she'd carried with her all day. With a plan forming in her mind, she strolled out of the storeroom toward Stefan and the woman she hoped would be a potential buyer.

Minutes later, having examined the clock in the crate, Mrs. Manford was gushing, "It's just magnificent."

Beside her, Stefan beamed as if he and not a seventeenth-century craftsman had made the clock.

"I've been looking for something to donate to the museum. Won't they love this, Stefan?" Mrs. Manford said bubblingly.

"Yes, they most certainly will."

Agreeably, Allie nodded in turn, pleased the clock would find a worthy home.

She watched as, minutes later, Stefan ushered the elated Mrs. Manford out the door.

It never closed behind them.

When Riley walked in, Allie nearly dropped the salt dish in her hand. Her stomach somersaulting, she braced herself for the unknown while he worked his way around two women in the aisle.

"I need to talk to you." He glanced at the customers still milling around the store, even though it was almost closing time. "I know you're busy, but this is important."

Tension knotted her stomach. "If you're wondering about all my things at your place, I'll phone a mover," she said, stepping away. "Just give me until tomorrow to—"

"I called my brother," he interrupted.

She froze in place. "You called him?" With emotions teetering close to the surface, she slid from one to another with lightning speed. Pleasure for Riley swept through her. Her caring, her love for him couldn't be shoved aside with the swiftness of some magician's wand. "What happened to him?" she asked.

"He's doing fine. Nice guy." Her smile made his decision to call Brandon seem even more right. "He was placed in foster care, but he was lucky. It was a good family. He lives in Colorado now." *And he doesn't blame me.*

Aware of the struggle he'd gone through to make that call, Allie wanted to hug him. "I'm glad you phoned him."

"So am I. I called my sister, too, to tell her that he and I would come to see her." That call to her had been harder. She'd cried, appealing to him to forgive her for unfairly blaming him. He'd been stunned by her words, ones of exoneration that he'd longed to hear two years ago, ones he'd needed to hear. But those weren't the words that had touched him most. "I love you," she'd said softly. That had nearly torn him apart.

"Oh, Riley." Something wonderful had happened to him, Allie realized.

"Yeah, it felt good." He gave her a smile, but felt as nervous as some adolescent kid on his first date. More than making a good impression was at stake. "Finding out they're both okay was..." He stopped, unable to express the relief, the satisfaction he'd felt. "It helped."

Allie looked past him to see Carol approach.

"I'm sorry to bother you again, Allie, but that gentleman over there—" she gestured with her head "—is a representative for Mrs. Sedwick. He's come to pick up the Rosenthal porcelain figures she purchased. I didn't know where you'd put them, or I would have—"

"It's all right, Carol. They're in the storeroom. I'll get them." Nervousness swarming in on her, Allie hurried to the back of the store. Riley looked more at peace with himself, she decided. Melodramatic thinking or not, she knew he'd had a tortured soul. She wondered what had finally made him make those phone calls. She would never know, she knew. He couldn't have changed so much in one day that he'd let her be part of him, be as one with him.

Veering toward the boxes in the storeroom, Allie noticed in passing, that her mother had given Devin a cookie and made herself a cup of tea.

"Riley's here?" Janet asked as she lifted her teacup.

"Yes." Allie reached behind a crate for Mrs. Sedwick's box.

The sound of footsteps made her look behind her.

"I came for that," Carol said helpfully.

Allie felt trapped. She wanted to be alone, but out there was Riley, in here her mother. Allie passed the box to Carol as her mother returned her empty teacup to the sink.

"I thought I'd take Devin to the park for a little while," Janet said.

"He'll like that." Allie reached for Devin and kissed his cheek.

"Say bye-bye to Mama," her mother urged.

He waved his fingers. "Bye."

Holding Devin in one arm, Janet gathered her purse and the diaper bag with the other. "Allie?"

Allie stiffened. As emotionally drained as she was, she couldn't deal with more advice.

"One question. And you don't have to answer me," her mother said, making Allie look back at her with puzzlement. "Are you the one who forced the moment between you and Riley last night?"

True to her words, she didn't wait for a response.

Allie watched them leave. *Oh, Mother, you do have a way with words.* Like before, she realized she *had* forced the moment last night. Why? Knowing Riley's pain, why hadn't she fought harder for them to stay together? The answer seemed simple suddenly. She'd pushed him away so she could leave him before he left her. Quite a revelation, she mused, and she sensed why. After the previous talk with her mother, she'd become aware of how much her father's leaving had touched her. Leaving Riley first meant not feeling abandoned.

"Did you forget me?" Riley asked, standing in the doorway with Devin in his arms. He waited for her eyes to meet his before he explained why he had the boy. "I ran into Janet and took him from her." As Allie stepped near, appearing to need her son in her arms, he carefully passed Devin to her. "I have more to say."

As if he hadn't spoken, she moved toward the cupboard and dug a cracker for Devin from an open box.

Riley geared up for another of the hardest yet most important moments of his life. His whole existence hinged on him convincing her he wasn't as dumb a jerk as he'd made her believe. "I figure two out of three Garrisons are on the right track now," he said, referring to his brother and sister. "That leaves only me with a problem." It's now or never, he reminded himself. "I know what I said to you. But you—and Devin—deserve a promise. I'll be here whenever either of you need me."

Allie acknowledged his words with a nod of her head. For someone who felt as he did about attachments, that was a giant concession, she knew. "Thank you."

The ridiculously polite conversation annoyed him. He wanted to shake her, make her look at him. "A lot of the problem between us had to do with other people, not with you." He braced a shoulder against the doorjamb. "I lied to myself for a lot of years, Allie."

Those weren't words she'd expected. She set Devin down to eat his cracker and rested her backside against the edge of the table.

"I wiped my brother and sister out of my life." Even now, even after the contact with them, Riley felt a heavy burden of guilt. He wasn't sure he'd ever convince himself that he hadn't failed them. On heavy legs, he crossed to the counter near her. Only a foot separated them now, but a lot more than distance kept them apart. "I was really dodging something else. I kept fooling myself, saying I didn't want involvement because I didn't want to screw up again."

Sadness for him floated up within her. So much of the guilt he'd carried had been unwarranted.

"That's what I told myself when you came into my life. That's how I convinced myself to keep you from getting too close. It was a lie. A nice, noble-sounding lie,'' he said with a trace of disgust.

"A lie?'' Allie's heart stopped. If blaming himself wasn't what had kept them apart, then her mother was wrong about everything.

"It's easier to pretend you're protecting someone else than it is to admit—to admit you're afraid.''

Allie's heart gave a tug—for him, for the pride she knew he'd buried to say those words.

Desperate now, he ached to touch her. For nearly two decades he'd shunned all happiness because of one emotion that clawed at him like some demon. He knew now that he'd been ripped open by fear. "I believed I didn't want a family, didn't want people to care about me, to rely on me. But the bottom line was that I didn't want to care, didn't want to love. Didn't want to lose again.'' Tentatively he pushed strands of hair away from her face. "Can you understand that?''

Too well, Allie mused. She'd been afraid, too, of something she hadn't been aware of. Instead of fighting for Riley's love, she'd backed away too easily because she'd been afraid he'd leave her like her father had.

"I didn't want anyone to need me. After my parents died, the kids were all I had. Then they were gone. And I started running, not from the responsibilities, but from emotion, from loving someone again.''

Allie bit her top lip, aware he was laying himself open to her.

"I met this woman who mattered too much.''

Strain colored his voice. "And what I felt for her scared the daylights out of me." With those beautiful, dark eyes on him, he stalled and drew a hard breath. "Allie, we could start over. This time we could make a commitment to each other, a real commitment. This time we could get married, do it for keeps."

He left her speechless, and her heart pounding as if it would burst through her chest. Two years ago, she'd waited to hear him say that word to her, she'd longed to hear that word. Allie stared down at Devin. "Why are you mentioning it now?" she made herself ask. "Because it's the right thing to do?" As much as she wanted to give Devin what Riley what was offering, marriage was just a piece of paper. She wanted his love.

Three words. He'd never said them. She was greedy, she knew. But until she heard those words, she couldn't marry him. She might have peeled away several layers and exposed emotions he'd hidden within him, but the heart of the man she loved still escaped her. No matter how much she wanted to be his wife, she couldn't settle for less.

Done with his cracker, Devin was punching at the buttons of a toy telephone. "Ello. Ello."

With her silence, Riley reined in frustration. "Devin deserves a father."

"You're saying this because of Devin then?" She couldn't stand living with Riley day in and day out, believing that if Devin didn't exist he would never have asked her to marry him. "I know how you feel about marriage, Riley."

"No, you don't," he said with a trace of annoyance. "How could you when I didn't know how I really felt myself?" Deliberately he softened his voice. "Listen, I don't blame you if you don't believe this turnaround," he said, trying again. "But answer one question first. You said you love me. Do you really?"

How could she say no? "Yes, I love you."

No hesitation, Riley thought with relief. Her words kick-started his heart. Taking a chance, he closed the last few inches between them and with unsteady hands touched her shoulders. No more shield. No more pulling away from her. "I need you. I want to be a permanent part of your life and Devin's. I want something from you that I've never wanted from anyone. I want you to need me," he whispered fiercely. "I never imagined that the one thing I've always denied wanting was what I need most." He framed her face with his hands. "I need love. I need a family."

Lightly he smoothed a thumb over her cheek. "Damn, you have no idea what you two mean to me. Let me love you. 'Cause I do." There was no one for him but her and the boy they'd made with that love. "I love you more than I want to admit. I love Devin."

Allie searched his eyes. Warm, intense emotion moved through her. He was telling her what she'd thought she'd never hear. "Say that again to me, that you love us," Allie murmured, but she was already stepping into his arms.

"I love both of you." He pressed his cheek against her hair. "The words don't seem enough."

They were enough for her. A smile sprang to her face as joy filled her. She raised her mouth to his, but only when she felt an acceptance in the lips moving over hers did she really allow herself to believe.

"Up," a small voice intruded before their kiss deepened.

Her arms snug around Riley's waist, Allie looked down with a soft laugh. Beside her, Devin had latched onto her leg. "I love your daddy," she said, then bent over to lift Devin into her arms.

Riley waited only until his son's smiling eyes were level with his. Resting one hand on Allie's waist and one on his son's small back, he brought them both closer. His heart open, willingly he welcomed them in. "I'll ask again. Will you marry me? Yes or no?" he said with impatience, because *he* needed the commitment from *her*.

Laughter bubbled in her throat. The brisk, no-nonsense and typically Riley manner stirred her smile. "How could I resist," she whispered, "when you ask so sweetly?"

"Be sure. Because it's forever," Riley insisted against her mouth.

Happiness and love poured out of her that he was finally giving her the greatest gift of all. He was trusting her with his heart. "Forever," Allie said softly, before her lips answered his in a celebration of the heart. She had more good news to tell him, but it could wait. Nothing could rival the joy within her at knowing they really would all be together—now and always.

Riley felt his throat tighten as he grasped how close he'd come to losing both of them. Overwhelmed, he shut his eyes and held her and Devin tightly to him, absorbing the taste of her lips against his, the warm flutter of his son's breath on his cheek. So much had been missing from his life. He had it all now.

He'd found more than a man hoped for when that one special woman entered his life.

He'd found a son.

He'd found a family.

* * * * *

♥™ SILHOUETTE

⟩SPECIAL EDITION⟨®

COMING NEXT MONTH

TENDERLY Cheryl Reavis

That Special Woman!

Wealthy Eden Trevoy is desperately seeking the truth about her lost heritage. But her searching reveals more than the hidden past as she captures the heart of Navajo policeman, Ben Toomey.

FINALLY A BRIDE Sherryl Woods

Always a Bridesmaid!

Katie Jones is finally getting married, the only hitch is that husband-to-be, Luke Cassidy has business—not love—on his mind. So, it's up to Katie to convince Luke to swap business for lifelong pleasure!

THE RANCH STUD Cathy Gillen Thacker

Hasty Weddings

Patience McKendrick has just come into an unusual inheritance. Knowing she's desperate for a baby, her eccentric uncle Max has left her handsome Josh Colter to sire her a child! But will she take her own advice and throw caution to the wind?

LITTLE BOY BLUE Suzannah Davis

Switched at Birth

Bliss Abernathy is stranded with her old foe, exasperating, but thrilling, Logan Campbell. But, once bitten, twice shy and Bliss is not about to lose her heart to Logan for a second time. After all, once they got back home everything would return to normal, wouldn't it?

DADDY'S HOME Pat Warren

When town bad boy Sam Rivers skipped town under a cloud of suspicion, he also left heiress Liza Courtland pregnant. Now Sam is back, but how can Liza let him be a part of her and her daughter's life after he has abandoned them once before?

HER CHILD'S FATHER Christine Flynn

Trapped by the weather with reclusive Jack Holt, Carrie Carter never dreamed that their isolation would lead to passion. But now Carrie is expecting Jack's baby, and it is up to her to break through Jack's reserve—for the sake of their child!

COMING NEXT MONTH FROM

 **SILHOUETTE®**

Intrigue
Danger, deception and desire

HER HERO Aimée Thurlo
FORGET ME NOT Cassie Miles
FLASHBACK Terri Herrington
HEART OF THE NIGHT Gayle Wilson

Desire
Provocative, sensual love stories for the woman of today

THE COWBOY STEALS A LADY Anne McAllister
BRIDE OF THE BAD BOY Elizabeth Bevarly
THE EDUCATION OF JAKE FLYNN Leandra Logan
HER TORRID TEMPORARY MARRIAGE Sara Orwig
THE KIDNAPPED BRIDE Metsy Hingle
THREE-ALARM LOVE Carole Buck

Sensation
A thrilling mix of passion, adventure and drama

CAPTIVE STAR Nora Roberts
A MARRIAGE-MINDED MAN Linda Turner
BRANDON'S BRIDE Alicia Scott
KNIGHT ERRANT Marilyn Pappano

EMILIE RICHARDS

THE WAY BACK HOME

As a teenager, Anna Fitzgerald fled an impossible situation, only to discover that life on the streets was worse. But she had survived. Now, as a woman, she lived with the constant threat that the secrets of her past would eventually destroy her new life.

1-55166-399-6
**AVAILABLE IN PAPERBACK
FROM SEPTEMBER, 1998**

JASMINE CRESSWELL

THE DAUGHTER

Maggie Slade's been on the run for seven years now.
Seven years of living without a life or a future because
she's a woman with a past. And then she meets Sean
McLeod. Maggie has two choices. She can either run,
or learn to trust again and prove her innocence.

"Romantic suspense at its finest."

—Affaire de Coeur

1-55166-425-9
AVAILABLE IN PAPERBACK
FROM SEPTEMBER, 1998

CHRISTIANE HEGGAN

SUSPICION

Kate Logan's gut instincts told her that neither of her
clients was guilty of murder, and homicide detective
Mitch Calhoon wanted to help her prove it. What neither suspected was how dangerous the truth would be.

*"Christiane Heggan delivers a tale that will leave you
breathless."*

—Literary Times

1-55166-305-8
**AVAILABLE IN PAPERBACK
FROM SEPTEMBER, 1998**

4 FREE

books and a surprise gift!

We would like to take this opportunity to thank you for reading this Silhouette® book by offering you the chance to take FOUR more specially selected titles from the Special Edition™ series absolutely FREE! We're also making this offer to introduce you to the benefits of the Reader Service™—

★ FREE home delivery
★ FREE gifts and competitions
★ FREE monthly newsletter
★ Books available before they're in the shops
★ Exclusive Reader Service discounts

Accepting these FREE books and gift places you under no obligation to buy; you may cancel at any time, even after receiving your free shipment. Simply complete your details below and return the entire page to the address below. *You don't even need a stamp!*

YES! Please send me 4 free Special Edition books and a surprise gift. I understand that unless you hear from me, I will receive 6 superb new titles every month for just £2.50 each, postage and packing free. I am under no obligation to purchase any books and may cancel my subscription at any time. The free books and gift will be mine to keep in any case.

E8YE

Ms/Mrs/Miss/Mr.................................Initials ....
BLOCK CAPITALS PLEASE

Surname ....

Address ....

....

....Postcode....................................

Send this whole page to:
THE READER SERVICE, FREEPOST, CROYDON, CR9 3WZ
(Eire readers please send coupon to: P.O. BOX 4546, DUBLIN 24.)

JAYNE ANN KRENTZ

A Woman's Touch

He was her boss—and her lover!
Life had turned complicated for Rebecca Wade when she
met Kyle Stockbridge. He *almost* had her believing he
loved her, until she realised she was in possession
of something he wanted.

"...one of the hottest writers in romance today."

—USA Today

1-55166-315-5
**AVAILABLE IN PAPERBACK
FROM AUGUST, 1998**